LOVERS LIKE US

MARY CAMPISI

MARY CAMPISI BOOKS, LLC

INTRODUCTION

Unlock the secrets in Reunion Gap

The only woman he's ever trusted is about to betray him…

Luke Donovan is the irresistible bad boy every woman wants, and no woman can catch. Until he meets Helena Montrey. There's something about her reserved manner and fresh-faced beauty that makes him *want* to commit…to her. Damn, but he's finally fallen in love! It's time to face up to past mistakes and returning to his hometown of Reunion Gap and the family he deserted is the first step.

After her fiancé's betrayal makes her question her ability to tell an honest man from a liar, Helena Montrey shies away from men. Then she meets Luke Donovan. Her heart wants to tell him she's the creator of a very successful greeting card line, not the struggling waitress and wannabe-writer he thinks she is. But her brain forces her to wait until she's sure the former bad boy with an admitted penchant for the open roads and constant change, is in this for keeps.

When the couple arrives in Reunion Gap, the Donovans are waiting for them with a lot of questions, and a ton of concerns. How is it that a woman they've never heard of ends up with a man who's vowed he'll never be tied down? What's the woman's back story? More importantly, what is she hiding? The truth about Helena will come out, and then Luke must decide if he loves her enough to give her a second chance.

The Donovans aren't going to stand by and watch this heartbreak happen without getting involved. After all, what's family for, if not to get involved?

Reunion Gap series:

Book One: *Strangers Like Us*
Book Two: *Liars Like Us*
Book Three: *Lovers Like Us*
Book Four: *Couples Like Us*
Book Five: *Guilty Like Us*

E-Book ISBN: 978-1-942158-39-4

Print ISBN: 978-1-942158-52-3

❀ Created with Vellum

An animal's love is pure, simple, absolute. This book is dedicated to everyone who has ever welcomed such unconditional love into their home and hearts.

R.I.P. Cooper Campisi, beloved rescue dog, most loyal friend and companion (2007-2018)

Chapter 1

Helena Montrey once created greeting cards about love and happily-ever-after until the man she planned to spend her life with broke her heart three weeks before their wedding. That's when she stopped believing in love, dreams, and a man's word. That's when she began creating greeting cards for the broken-hearted women and men who'd been jilted, cheated on, and tossed aside. She considered it therapy but the brother and sister who ran the business end of the greeting card company called it genius and more profitable than the feel-good love cards she'd once written.

The words came without effort, often in the middle of another sleepless night.

He stole your dreams...
She torched your soul...
There will be new dreams...
New hopes...
You will not let his actions define you...
She will not destroy you...
One day you will trust again...
One day you will open your heart to love again...
You will give trust another chance...

And life will shine...

OF COURSE, she didn't necessarily believe the part about trusting or loving again, but it *could* work for other people. Why not give them hope even if she had none left? Writing and creating became her therapy and for thirteen months she fell in and out of her days, pretending life was good, she was fine, better off without him.

She weathered news of her ex's engagement, marriage, and upcoming fatherhood with a straight face and a who-cares attitude, but each announcement required late-night wine, dark chocolate, and a box of tissues. There were moments between the wine and chocolate when she considered picking up the phone and calling him. But what would be the point? He'd fallen in love with another woman and it hadn't mattered that he'd been three weeks away from saying "I do" or that his shiny new wedding band lay tucked in his top dresser drawer. The dreams, the plans, the two children they'd share one day, all disappeared the second he told her he loved someone else.

To his credit, he'd never told Helena that he *didn't* love her, as though somehow not admitting that might make his confession more palatable—which, of course, it didn't. She'd been sitting on the couch, checking off last-minute details for the wedding when he'd stood over her, the voice she loved a mix of misery and apology.

Helena? We need to talk.

He'd never been one to drag out the inevitable, and within the span of a commercial break she knew all about the college sweetheart who just so happened to turn up a few months ago—the one Helena had never heard about—and heaven help him, the feelings resurfaced and couldn't be ignored or denied. That handsome face did look a bit contrite when he admitted he should have told her before but didn't know how.

She might have believed the tale if he hadn't slipped in the part about Helena buying *him* out of the house she'd recently added his name to—the house *she'd* bought, the mortgage *she'd* paid, the one he'd persuaded her to add his name to and which she'd done, thanks to her trusting nature. And stupidity. A whole lot of stupidity.

But there'd been more. He'd driven off in the new sports car she'd given him, an early wedding present from the bride who was not going to be his bride. He'd taken the car, the house, the stacks of vinyl albums, and the closetful of hand-tailored suits she'd bought him. And he'd been quite clever about not signing for anything wedding-related, so Helena ended up paying for the balance of the nuptials that didn't take place. The more he took, the more she realized their relationship had never been about love, marriage, or a happily-ever-after—at least not with her. The man who had the sweetest compliments and an answer for absolutely everything had played her. He'd looked into her eyes and when he spoke, she'd believed every single word.

Even if they were all lies.

The day she learned the truth about her fiancé and the deceit that lives in a person's soul was the day she decided no man would ever get close enough to hurt her again.

And then she met Luke Donovan.

PEOPLE CALLED HIM RECKLESS, wild, and unpredictable, but Lucas John Donovan liked to think of himself as a man who wouldn't be tied down by a job, a belief, or a woman. He liked staying open to new challenges, hopping in his truck and heading down the road to an as-yet-unknown destination. Getting stuck in one place, tied to one woman was an oxygen drain for sure. It wasn't that he was opposed to either—hell, he'd even consider a relationship if the woman was the right one. But that was the problem.

How would he ever know when the right one came along? They all felt "right for now" but what about tomorrow and the day after that? What about long-term? Waking up next to that same person for the rest of his life? Listening to her yammer in his ear about this or that, making demands on his time? And the expectations that would come with it? The dinners with people he didn't know or couldn't stand, the compliments he'd have to force out of his mouth, the sharing that would be part of the deal. Yeah, that was something he couldn't picture.

He'd lost a few buddies when they found "the one," and some of them had even gotten married and had a kid. They'd traded in Saturday night drinking and Sunday football for prime time with their one-and-only. Okay, so they didn't have to go looking for sex but then neither did Luke. It always found him. Sure, if his friends got sick there was somebody to feed them chicken soup and nag about drinking hot tea. Well, he had a mother for that and while she might be hundreds of miles away, if he needed a mother, he knew where to find her.

Luke might be considered a "bad influence" by the wives but most thought all he needed was the right woman to make him respectable. In other words, sleep in the same bed with the same woman, have a kid or two, move to the suburbs, learn to grill chicken instead of red meat, and don't forget to put down the toilet seat. The wives didn't miss an opportunity to introduce candidates for his transformation. Why would a woman introduce her friend to a guy with a love-'em-and-leave-'em reputation? *Unless* she really believed her choice could change him.

Right. Not happening.

But every once in a while, he did wonder if there was someone out there who might make him *want* to be different, want to be a better person. He'd even agreed to meet a few of the prospective candidates, but it always ended the same: the friend fell for him, he broke her heart, and the wife forbid him from stepping foot in her house again. Still, his buddies warned that one day he'd meet a woman who could break *his* heart, and then he'd know *she* was the one. That made no sense at all—until the day it happened.

Later, he'd like to say it was the hot-and-sour soup that brought them together and the killer cold that stole his breathing *and* his logic, but she'd called it *destiny*. And he'd have to agree. His mother believed homemade chicken soup helped a cold but since she was a plane ride away, he'd have to depend on the hot-and-sour soup his buddy insisted would do the trick. Luke bundled up and drove to the Chinese restaurant a few blocks away, a dark place with Asian music and tiny candles on the tables. He thought he heard a waterfall in the distance but that could have been part of the music filtering through the speakers. Luke didn't know, and he didn't care. All he wanted was soup and tea and a nose he could breathe through.

A man who looked like he'd been around as long as the old cash register sitting on the counter peered at Luke from behind round wire-rimmed glasses and motioned him to a small table in the corner of the restaurant. The man smiled, revealing two rows of crooked teeth, and pointed to an empty chair. "Sit," he said in broken English. "Wait." Then he turned and headed toward the kitchen, his small frame blending into the darkness. Luke shrugged out of his jacket, eased onto the chair, and closed his eyes. Maybe he'd buy an extra container of soup to eat later... He massaged his temples, sipped air through his mouth.

"Are you okay?"

Luke opened his eyes, blinked. The vision before him blurred, settled into place. It was a woman: tall, dark-haired, lots of curves. He blinked again, wiped a hand over his forehead. "Bad cold. Can I get some hot-and-sour soup?"

"Sure. Would you like tea? Or an egg roll with hot mustard?" She smiled, and he noticed dimples on either side of her cheeks. "The hot mustard will open you up. No doubt about it."

He nodded. "Okay. Tea and the egg roll." He squinted at her, added, "And the mustard."

"I'll be right back."

Luke watched her walk away, noticed the sway of her full hips, the bounce of her long hair against her shoulder blades... He must have dozed off because the next thing he heard was the woman's voice next to him.

"Here's your tea, soup, and the egg roll. Make sure you add a healthy dollop of the hot mustard."

Her smile made her eyes sparkle. What color were they? Amber? Green? Luke tried to tell but the lighting was too dark, and he was too sick. "Thanks." He dunked the egg roll in the hot mustard, bit into it, and thought his head would explode. Luke snatched the glass of water, chugged it down, stared at the woman. "I could've used a warning."

"I'm so sorry. I guess you have to build up a tolerance."

"Yeah. Guess so." He shook his head, sipped the hot-and-sour soup, kept his gaze on the woman. He wished it weren't so dark in here so he could get a better look at her; she sounded nice and genuine and he wanted to see what that looked like when he wasn't in hunting mode.

"The soup should help, and if you'll give the mustard another try, that should, too."

"So, dip it, don't coat it?" He lifted the egg roll, dipped the end in the hot mustard. His nose had started to clear and there'd been a few seconds when the stuffiness had disappeared.

She smiled. "Right."

Luke eyed the restaurant, noticed there was only one other customer. "Can I buy you a drink? Tea? Or maybe an egg roll with hot mustard?"

The woman laughed. "No thanks. I've already had my quota for the day."

He liked talking with her even if it was about how to unstuff his nose and clear his head. "Do you want to sit down for a minute?" he asked, motioning to the chair opposite him. "I mean, if you won't get into trouble—" he paused, added "—and if you aren't worried about catching my cold..."

There was a second of hesitation before she slid back the chair and sat. "It's slow and I didn't take a break today. I'll sit for a minute."

"Good." He dipped the rest of the egg roll in the hot mustard, popped it in his mouth, and let the mustard do its work. "I'm Luke."

"Helena."

No last names but when had it become necessary to attach a last name with the waitress who served him? Hell, there'd been too many times when a woman had delivered a lot more than food and he'd never gotten her last name. There'd even been a time or two when he hadn't gotten her first. He pushed that last truth away, concentrated on the woman across from him. Damn, but he wished it weren't so hot in here and his head weren't so foggy. She fell out of focus and Luke squinted. Almond-shaped eyes, arched brows...what color were her eyes? More squinting, but he couldn't tell.

She eyed him and when she spoke, her words could have been a lecture if the tone hadn't been so soft. "At the risk of sounding like a mother, you know you should be home in bed, drinking fluids, and resting."

He managed a smile, decided he liked the way she delivered a suggestion. "You do sound like a mother." Pause. "*My* mother."

"I like to think of it as common sense, a trait most men don't have when they're sick."

"Ah, a woman with a quick tongue. Sorry, but my brain's too fuzzy right now to keep up." He coughed, tried to clear his throat, coughed again. "So, are you from here?"

She shrugged, looked away. "I'm just passing through. You?"

"Same. I'm with a building crew; we travel the country, work projects, and move on."

"Houses?"

He nodded. "I've done everything from roofing to drywall and plumbing. Carpentry's my specialty."

"And you just keep moving? No place to call home?"

What to say to that? Maybe it was the cold or the fever that made him extra chatty, but bits of truth slipped out that he usually guarded. "I like Colorado, and I've done a lot of work here, but my home's in Pennsylvania. It's a small town called Reunion Gap. I don't get there often but it'll always be home."

"Maybe you'll settle down there someday," she said, her voice soft, curious.

Luke shrugged. "Maybe." There was a lot of doubt in that word, considering how he and his sister had dumped their parents' problems on their oldest brother. Luke should have helped; he should not have pretended he was too busy to do the right thing. He'd been too self-absorbed and unwilling to accept the unpleasantness of his parents' situation, and now he had to live with those actions. "What about you? Where do you call home?"

He didn't miss the slight hesitation before she spoke, followed by an extra breath of air that said her next words might not be one hundred percent accurate, or if they were, she wished they weren't.

"San Diego."

She didn't sound happy about it and if he weren't feeling so miserable he might have poked around a bit for details. "I've been there. Nice place."

"That's what everybody says."

But what about you? he wanted to ask. *Do you think it's a nice place? And if you don't, why?* Of course, he wasn't sick enough to forget his manners, so he let the comment slide and pretended he hadn't heard the edge in her voice that said the place didn't feel like home. "So, how'd you end up working here?" That should be an easy question with a simple answer, except it wasn't. Nope, the answer she gave him wasn't an answer at all...

"I started working here because of the food." She met his gaze, held it, finished with "What can I say? I love moo goo gai pan."

They didn't meet again until five days later when Luke's head was clear, and his brain was synapsing. The woman had occupied his thoughts during waking and sleeping hours since he met her, and he wanted to see her again. No doubt the obsession had more to do with his debilitated state and less to do with reality, and he planned to find out. Actually, he planned to confirm his suspicions that the cold meds and the foggy brain were the reason for his altered reality.

But once he saw her again, he had to admit he'd been dead wrong.

The attraction was real and the heat between them had nothing to do with the coffeehouse's fireplace. The look on Helena's face when she spotted him said she felt it too and was just as surprised, and from the frown, just as perplexed. Maybe that's why she'd nixed his offer for dinner and recommended coffee instead. Tame. Easy. Noncommittal. Yeah, that's what he'd do if he were trying to get a bead on another person and make sure she didn't get the wrong impression about accepting an invitation. She'd even bought her own coffee before he showed up. Nothing like making sure he understood this was not a date—or anything. Luke ordered a coffee, unzipped his jacket, and made his way to the leather chair next to hers.

"Hey. I could have sprung for your coffee."

Helena eyed him. "And I could have sprung for yours if I'd known what you like."

Ah, a woman with attitude. He laughed, sank into the chair, and set his coffee on the table between them. "Black, the strongest they've got."

"I'm not surprised."

"I'm guessing you're a sugar, splash of cream kind of girl?"

Her laughter shot through him, made a beeline to his crotch. "Black, the strongest they've got." The laughter faded. "You seem to have recovered from your cold."

"Back to normal." Her eyes were amber, like a bourbon neat.

"You were a lot less intimidating the other day with your raspy voice and your hair sticking out all over the place. Unshaven, dressed in sweat pants with a cough that threatened to contaminate the whole restaurant."

He shrugged, tried to ignore the heat creeping up his neck. "Yeah, that was not my best moment." Luke rubbed his jaw, slid his gaze to her. "And yet you helped me."

"You reminded me of a stray puppy I once rescued."

"I see." This woman was never going to let his head swell, that was for sure. Unlike the usual ones who couldn't wait to tell him how perfect he was, movie-star handsome and sexy as hell. Of course, it was all a setup for whatever they wanted from him. But this one seemed different and that intrigued the hell out of him.

"I didn't mean that as an insult; it's just that I enjoyed talking with you the other night. There was no subterfuge, no come-ons...just talking." Her smile pulled out the dimples on either side of her cheeks. "When you weren't coughing or sputtering from a hot-mustard jolt. It was refreshing." She paused, said in a quiet voice, "And that's why I accepted the invitation to coffee. Usually, I would just say thanks but no thanks."

And why was that? He wanted to know, wondered if something had happened to turn her off men. She was probably in her late twenties, a few years younger than he was, but old enough to have gotten blown up by a relationship and a guy. "I'm glad you didn't." If they were sharing partial truths, he might as well offer one of his own. "My friends' wives have been trying to match me up with the perfect woman who they swear will change my life. Not that I've asked them to, but they've decided it's what I need."

"How's it worked out for you?"

Luke winced. "Not well. I've been uninvited to almost all my friends' houses. Their wives say I'm a bad influence who needs taming."

"Are they wrong?"

The question slipped between his defenses, hovered like a butterfly waiting to land. "The expectations were wrong." He met her gaze, admitted the truth. "The women were wrong, too. Finding the right one is the key. I never believed that before, but...the premise has value, I see that now." Helena sipped her coffee, stared at the fire as though contemplating what he'd said. There was so much he didn't know about her and for the first time in his life, he was curious enough to want to stick around and find out more. Was that crazy? Was *he* crazy? He'd only just met her...

"Why are you really here, Luke?" She dragged her gaze to his, offered a sad smile. "If it's to sleep with me, you've picked the wrong person."

"I want to get to know you, Helena. When I met you the other night, I felt a connection, even with a world-class cold and foggy brain. I think you felt it, too." He waited for her to deny it and when she didn't he continued. "You've haunted me since that night and I had to see you again to make sure it wasn't the cold meds or the fever playing games with me." His voice dipped. "It wasn't."

She bit her bottom lip, blinked hard. "That is not what I want to hear."

"But?"

"You're right...there was a ...connection of some sort."

Not a joy-filled acknowledgment, but he'd take it. "Okay, then."

"Okay, then?" Her brows pinched together. "What does that mean?"

Luke stretched out his legs, crossed his booted feet at the ankles, and said, "That means we'll get to know each other...nice and slow...you set the rules and the groundwork. I'll follow your lead." He reached across the small table, clasped her hand. "And we'll see where it takes us."

Chapter 2

A woman should never believe a man like Luke whose last name she didn't know when he told her he'd take it slow and let her set the pace. What he really meant was he'd use his easygoing charm and soft-talking persuasion to convince her she didn't *want* to go slow...or pace herself. He would get her so spun up that *she'd* be the one doing the undressing and touching, she'd be the one who broke the rules and took *him* to bed—even though she knew she shouldn't.

And that's exactly what happened though she'd be lying if she said she regretted it. A woman didn't regret a night with a man like Luke; she prayed for more. Helena tried not to notice the way her belly fluttered when he spoke her name or the heat that swirled through her when she caught those pale blue eyes watching her. The man was too darn handsome: the perfect nose, the full lips, the golden highlights streaking curls the color of whiskey. And she did not want to think about the tanned and toned body because it was just too distracting, and she was not going to be distracted by any man.

Unless that man looked like the stranger who'd coughed and sniffed his way into her life less than a week ago. Then, she had to reconsider. *I don't even know your last name*, she'd said when he asked her to dinner that night at the coffeehouse.

Donovan, he'd murmured, his lips pulling into a slow smile. *Lucas John Donovan. What else do you want to know?* He'd closed the distance between them, cupped her chin with his thumb and forefinger, and placed a breathtakingly soft kiss on her lips.

What else did she want to know? Nothing, because her brain couldn't function. He must have known because he pulled back, traced her lips with his fingers and whispered, *Just give me your address and I'll pick you up tomorrow at 6:00.*

Helena should have told him she'd changed her mind or given him a fake address, but she hadn't. Oh no. Not only had she provided him with her real address, she'd given him her cell phone number. Did that not say *desperate* and dying to see you again?

She wasn't desperate, but she *did* want to see Luke Donovan again and there was no pretending she didn't. It had been thirteen months since her fiancé killed her dreams when he admitted he was in love with someone else. That was a long time to let pain devour her, wasn't it? Trust would not come easy or fast, but perhaps she could begin a vetting process of sorts: make sure Luke Donovan cared about *her* and not her money, determine if he really could invest in a relationship with one woman. If he passed the test, well then, who knew what might happen?

Unfortunately, it was the unknown that petrified her and the fact that she might not be objective where this man was concerned. How could she be when his fresh scent filled the cab of the truck, his voice seeping into her brain, his long fingers just a touch away? They'd dined at a local steakhouse and talked about food, movies, country music, the town. He shared the exhilaration of skydiving, the adventures of hiking through the Rockies, and the peace that comes in the black of night. She talked about volunteering at an animal shelter, finding the perfect cup of coffee, and how music calmed her. When she told him she wrote greeting cards on the side and had even sold a few, he'd called her brave and talented.

If he only knew the truth.

But how could she tell him she and her two siblings had inherited the greeting card company from their parents, or that she'd created the Annabelle Grace card line when she was still in college? That bit of information sharing would highlight the fact that she had money and lots of it. She'd once again become the perfect target for a man set on increasing his wealth through acquisition of a woman, namely her assets. It was much too soon to admit those truths...but she wasn't the only one holding back. The hesitancy behind Luke's words told her there was a chunk of his personal life he hadn't owned up to either. Maybe they were both waiting to see if the other person would earn the right to learn them.

They left the steakhouse and Luke drove her back to the apartment she was subleasing. He parked the truck, turned to her. "I've never met a woman who was easier to talk to than you are." His full lips pulled into a slow smile. "You have a way of making a man feel like he's the only one on this earth."

Well, maybe that was because when Luke Donovan was near a woman, there *was* no other man breathing in her universe. Of course, she couldn't tell him that so she merely shrugged and said, "I know the feeling."

"Helena." His smile faded and he leaned toward her, kissed her.

She moaned against his lips, opened her mouth, and let him deepen the kiss. *So tempting. Mesmerizing. Delicious.* Helena broke the kiss. "This is really not a good idea." *But oh, how she wanted it.*

He planted a kiss on her right temple, held her gaze. "Nope."

She sucked in a breath, tried to think, but he was too close. "I don't go in for casual...acquaintances."

His voice dipped. "Good to know."

"And I'm not looking for long-term either."

"Uh-huh." He fingered the first button of her shirt.

She squirmed, tried to wriggle away. "Maybe you should stop." She cleared her throat, clasped her hands on his shoulders, and pulled him closer.

"Yeah." He unbuttoned the first button, dipped a finger inside the opening of her shirt, touched her flesh. "Maybe." He did stop before he reached the next button, eased away, and let out a long sigh. "I think you'd better go inside." His gaze burned into her, matched the heat in his voice when he asked, "Can I see you again?"

The sizzle between them made it impossible to say no.

Helena saw Luke the next two nights and at the end of each evening he walked her to the door, placed a soft kiss on her mouth, and headed to his own place—and his own bed. On the third night when he leaned down to kiss her, she flung her arms around his neck, pressed her body against his, and kissed him with all the passion and need she'd been storing up for so many months. "Come inside," she breathed against his lips.

Luke pulled away, met her gaze, his eyes bright under the glow of the moon. "Are you sure?"

Of course, she wasn't sure. The man created feelings inside her that were raw and deep and terrifying. But that wasn't going to stop her from giving him an answer. "Yes," she whispered, stroking his jaw.

He kissed her again, devoured her mouth, coaxing out tiny whimpers of need as he tasted, teased, and consumed her. When he broke the kiss, his eyes glittered, his voice turned hoarse. "Let's go inside."

They stayed in bed for two days, learning each other's body, talking and not talking. Sharing in a way she'd never imagined and certainly never experienced before, not even with her fiancé. And yet, here she was, naked, in bed with a man she hadn't known existed two weeks ago. Was she crazy? Desperate? Was any of this real or was it a fantasy that would end once they left the bed?

What if it didn't end? What if these feelings were real and Luke felt them, too?

Then what?

The next morning, Luke headed home to change clothes before work with a promise to make chicken fajitas for her tonight. Thoughts of spending the night with him, in and out of bed, made her belly jump in ways that had nothing to do with her morning caffeine. Luke Donovan had worked his way into her brain, her heart, *and* her bed, and if she didn't slow down, she'd never be able to observe him with an objective eye. How did one observe a person with objectivity when she was sleeping with him? When they were together, he treated her as though no other woman existed, but then didn't most players possess the capacity to do that?

At least he didn't know about her business or her financial position, but how long could she keep that a secret? Or rather, how long did she *want* to keep it a secret? She sipped her coffee and munched on a slice of peanut butter toast as she thought about the man who'd taken over huge chunks of her brain *and* her heart and shown no signs of leaving either one.

Helena grabbed a pad and started a grocery list for tonight's dinner. *Chicken breasts, red pepper, onions...* The phone interrupted her thoughts and she grabbed it, spotted her sister's number. "Hi, Estelle."

"Helena? What's going on? I've been trying to reach you since yesterday. Dominic and I were worried about you."

"Worried? I'm fine." *So much better than fine...*

Big sigh and a stern "Why can't you just come home?"

Were they really going to have this conversation again? "You know why. San Diego isn't my home anymore."

"Because of that jerk ex-fiancé who used you? You could move to the other side of the city and chances are you'd never run into him. Besides—" she let out a harsh laugh "—seems Mr. Cheater's perfect world is about to land on top of him. Guess he has a problem being second to a baby, even if the baby's his. And I hear the wife thinks real men change diapers and do the grocery shopping." More laughter. "Mr. Cheater apparently missed the seminar on what constitutes a good partner. Of course, he also missed the one on what constitutes a decent human being, but we already knew that."

"Estelle, I really don't care about him." She'd said that so many times and yet, this time, it really was true.

"Well, I do. I want to enjoy every detail of his crash-and-burn and when he lands in the ashes, I'll be the first one to cheer."

Helena rubbed her temple, tried to comprehend what her sister had just told her. "How do you know all of this? And *why* do you know it?" None of this made any sense unless her sister was projecting her dislike on the man and her desire to see him punished. Or she'd hired a private investigator to provide details. The last possibility clung to Helena, made her ask, "Did you hire someone to investigate him? Please tell me you didn't do that."

"Why not? I *did* have him investigated, and only wish I'd done it before the two of you became serious. Then we'd have known all about him and the other girlfriend, and that he was using you to get whatever he could, especially your money."

Estelle had never learned the art of protecting another person's feelings, especially Helena's. "Gee, thanks, I guess no man would ever want me for me." She meant to be sarcastic but a tiny piece of her believed the words, and maybe that was another reason she hadn't told Luke about her business *or* her money.

"That's not it at all, but you've always been too trusting and much too innocent where men are concerned. You wouldn't know a player or a con artist if he sat next to you. Dominic and I have to keep you safe; that's what family does."

That last part was debatable, at least in their family. Helena's siblings wanted to keep her in San Diego so they could make sure she kept producing the greeting cards that paid for their fancy lifestyles. But did they really care about *her*? Did they want her to be happy? "So, were you just checking in or..."

"Both," her sister said in a rushed voice. "Dominic and I have never liked you traipsing all over the country, but you said you needed the space to create. *Be a wanderer and open your heart to the world*, is what you said." She blew out a sigh of irritation. "You and Daddy were so alike. Mama said he was more comfortable living out of a hotel room than his own house, but at least she always knew where he was. But you? You could be in Anchorage, Alaska, or Mobile, Alabama, and nobody would know."

"That's ridiculous." Why was she being so melodramatic? Had something happened to upset her? "You always know where I'm headed, and I've always called you back within a few hours." *Except this time...because I was in bed with Luke Donovan.*

"Ha! Is that supposed to make us feel better? Do you have any idea how helpless that makes us feel? I should have listened to Dominic and hired someone to keep an eye on you."

"Hire someone? Don't you ever do that, or I swear I will not be happy and then see how many cards I create." Estelle was the marketing head of the company and Dominic was the business end, but they needed Helena to create, and when they tried to strong-arm their little sister, she reminded them of that not-so-insignificant fact.

"Oh, all right, calm down. We won't hire anyone." Silence followed by a softer inquiry. "Helena, where have you been?"

"Still in Colorado. Same small town."

"And you couldn't take a minute to call? I left several messages."

No, she really had not wanted to be disturbed. Luke Donovan had that effect on her. "I'm sorry. I was preoccupied..." She should keep quiet but what if her sister decided to hire that investigator? Then she'd find out about Luke and there'd be questions, and something told her Luke wouldn't be happy if anybody dug around in his business. "I'm working on a new project and I don't want to jinx it, but it's been taking over my life lately..."

His name is Luke Donovan.

He's tall, rugged, so handsome.

And he's consuming my every waking and sleeping moment.

"Oh." And then "I'll bet you're watching *Pride & Prejudice* for the seventy-fifth time, aren't you?"

Helena picked up her pen, doodled on the corner of the grocery list. Mr. Darcy had nothing on Luke Donovan. "Something like that."

"Okay. Good." Pause, another huff. "How is the inspiration going? Do you think you'll be home by the end of the month?"

That was only two weeks away. "Umm...I'm not sure." If she left then, what would happen with Luke? He'd told her he traveled with a crew and worked on houses, but what were the odds he'd end up in San Diego? Two weeks was not a lot of time to find out if there was more to "them" than sex and a few conversations. Okay, the sex was great, and the conversations were deep, but still, they didn't know each other very well...not well enough to ask a person to come to San Diego, or worse, try for a long-distance relationship. She hadn't even been able to manage a relationship with a guy in the same city, so how would this ever work?

Had Luke said anything about long-term?

Had he even hinted he'd like her to stick around?

Of course, he hadn't.

But then, neither had she.

"Helena? Is something wrong? You don't sound like yourself."

Her sister had a way of sniffing out Helena's emotional state, like a beagle on a hunt. "I'm fine. Really, no worries here. I'll be in touch."

Chapter 3

Luke bought a bouquet of pink roses and one of those mushy cards that talked about being happy when the other person was near, and how they were the other part of the whole. Whatever. It sounded good, and he thought Helena might like it. Actually, it was kind of how he felt even though he didn't want to admit it. He'd always been a man's man, tough and not given to flowery words or sentiment. If he cared about a woman, she'd know it, so he shouldn't have to spit out the niceties more than once. And love? He'd never used that word unless he was referring to a new tool or a football game. But with Helena, he had a feeling that things would be different.

He could probably get used to spitting out the words she wanted to hear, especially if she gave him that slow smile that said she wanted him to come closer so she could touch him. Yeah, a few smiles and a touch and he'd spew sentiments like a gusher.

This was all moving way too fast and he couldn't get a handle on what was happening or find a way to slow it down. Every time he was near Helena he wanted to touch her, talk to her, see her face light up the way it did when he said something she liked. Damn, he sounded like a puppy looking for a pat on the head. What was happening to him and how did he stop it? If his buddies could see him, they'd laugh him off the job site.

But so what?

He could play macho and act like he didn't care about Helena, but why?

For the first time in his life, he *did* care about a woman, really cared, and he wanted to be with her even though two weeks ago he hadn't known she existed. So what? Did it really matter? Did anything matter but being with her, getting to know her on such a deep level that she'd become part of him? The other half of the whole? Maybe that was all BS, or maybe it was real.

He didn't know, but he sure as hell wanted to find out. Luke grabbed his jacket, the card, and the bouquet of roses from the counter and headed out the door.

As the weeks passed, Luke knew he and Helena were meant to spend their lives together. She was an angel sent to transform his philandering ways and show him what true love meant. He wanted to commit to her and only her, and if she would give him an opportunity, he'd spend the rest of his life proving his worthiness.

Yes, he'd really said that.

All of it, and more.

She'd listened, those full lips quivering, the amber eyes rimmed with tears. And told him she felt the same.

Life was full, heaven was within reach, and they were going to grab it and spend the rest of their lives in total bliss. That's what he told her and some nights, that's what she told him. Maybe if he hadn't been so hypnotized by her presence, he'd have noticed the tiny inconsistencies: the hesitation when he asked about her family, the catch in her voice that preceded her responses, even the time or two she looked away. But he'd missed every single clue because he hadn't been looking for them.

Ten weeks after Luke walked into the Chinese restaurant, life surprised them with a pregnancy. Sure, the timetable wasn't ideal, but they loved each other and wasn't that all that really mattered? Yes, absolutely. They were going to share a child, a bond that would tie them together for the rest of their lives. Luke ignored the queasiness in his gut, bought a ring and proposed. The quiet civil ceremony followed two weeks later, along with a honeymoon weekend at a swanky ski resort. Marriage, a kid, a new life.

It would all be worth it as long as Helena was at his side.

But the moving from town to town, the dingy hotels and restaurant meals that had been part of his life for a lot of years? Those had to go. It was time to make decisions that weren't just based on what he wanted or didn't want. He had a wife and kid to think about.

They needed a home. Stability. They needed family and that's why they were headed back to his hometown. Helena hadn't been too keen on driving cross-country to meet a bunch of strangers even if they were his family. She'd worried they would judge—for the unplanned pregnancy, the quickie wedding, the snap decision to move back to Reunion Gap. How could he tell her that with a family like his, they'd be watching and drawing conclusions no matter what the circumstances?

While it hadn't been his first or second choice, he'd offered to head to San Diego to meet her brother and sister, maybe find a place nearby if she'd rather stay close to them. He'd never pictured himself settling down in a city but then he'd never pictured himself settling down at all, or meeting someone like Helena. It would be untrue to say he didn't feel relief when she declined the offer of a San Diego move or a meet-and-greet with her siblings. She said that could come in time and he didn't push for reasons, though later, he'd realize he should have.

For now, his thoughts were on heading home after a too-long absence with a wife and a baby on the way. That would create turmoil and a million questions. The turmoil he didn't mind; it was the questions he wanted to avoid. People would ask where he'd been, what he'd been doing, and why he hadn't come home to help when his father needed him. It was the last question they really wanted to know but they'd work their way up to it, and then wait for his answer. What could he say? Certainly not the truth; *I ran away because I didn't want to deal with their pain?* What kind of person does that? Not an honorable one, that was for sure.

And then the town would inquire about his new wife. She'd cause as much controversy and curiosity as the reason he hadn't returned home. The woman who'd won his heart *and* his name was not going to be welcomed in a town where he'd broken a lot of hearts, even if those hearts had not listened when he'd told them he was not a one-woman man.

But the worst of it would come from his own family. Not his mother, or his Aunt Camille or Uncle Oliver, but his brother and sister. Rogan and Charlotte would want details and confirmation that he really did love Helena and that he understood what that meant, as if he were an idiot. Rogan would no doubt lecture him on marriage and monogamy and how you didn't put that ring on your finger unless you could commit to both. Sure, let him talk, because Luke had never been more committed to anyone in his life.

Charlotte would probably want to have a chat with Helena, a.k.a., *interrogate* her and he could imagine his sister's questions. She'd never been one for subtlety and he doubted she'd refined her touch.

Where did you meet my brother?

What made you so sure he was the one?

Were you ever in a long-term relationship before?

Live-in? Married?

Can you see yourself with Luke twenty years from now?

When he walks into a room, do you find it hard to breathe?

Will you love him, no matter what?

And once she found out about the baby, the gloves would come off in her effort to protect him.

Did you trap my brother into marriage?

Did you want to get pregnant?

Are you sure you didn't trap him?

Why didn't you use protection?

Don't hurt my brother.

I mean it.

Do not hurt my brother.

His kid sister was a fighter, always had been even when it wasn't her battle, and Rogan was no different. He had a bit more polish than Charlotte, but he was all about protecting family, even the ones who'd disappointed him—like Luke.

He'd tried to prepare Helena for the Donovans and the small town where he'd grown up, but some things had to be experienced to be understood. Helena had eased up on her nervousness about meeting his family and said they could stay as long as he wanted. Hadn't she made a reference or two about settling down there, finding a home and being near his family?

She had no idea what she was saying. No idea at all. It would be a disaster. People would poke at their business every second, telling them what to do, what not to do, even why they should or shouldn't do it. Who needed that? But there was a small part of him that wondered what it would be like to drop in for a beer and conversation —if the conversation weren't about him.

It took four days to reach Reunion Gap. Luke's truck was a gas hog, but with an extended cab it was a lot more comfortable than Helena's compact, which they'd sold to one of the waiters at the restaurant. They'd probably have to trade in the truck and get some-thing more baby-friendly, maybe an SUV. Not a minivan. Good Lord, he was not ready for one of those. He guessed they'd have to talk about it, along with the hundreds of other considerations new parents discussed. It would have been a lot easier if they'd been a couple first and parents second, but when had he ever done anything the easy way?

They entered town early one February morning as snow coated the ground and the wind drove down the temperatures. He'd always loved winters in Reunion Gap: the landscape stripped bare, trees weighed down with ice and snow, the winds howling, Exposed. Raw. Danger-ous. His father had once said only the very brave or the very stupid ventured out in weather like this. Luke always figured he fit into the latter category because he was one of the first to volunteer to deliver groceries, plow driveways, and dig out cars that were buried in the snow. Was it noble? He never stopped to think about it. They were jobs that needed doing and who better to do them than a guy with no ties? No wife, no girlfriend...nothing to hold him back.

But now life was different. There was Helena and the baby, and he couldn't run off at the first sign of distress—his or anyone else's. He sucked in a breath, blew it out, and pulled into the driveway where the Donovan house stood, looking worn and sad, not much different from the last time he saw his father.

"Welcome to Reunion Gap," he said, easing the truck into Park, and clasping his wife's hand. Her smile made him forget how much he still didn't know about her. Luke leaned forward, placed a soft kiss on her lips. What else did he need to know? They loved each other; they'd figure it out as they went along...

HELENA CLUTCHED Luke's arm and held tight as they made their way to the front porch of the weathered farmhouse. He'd tried to reassure her that the areas had been plowed and there was no danger of slipping, but that wasn't her issue. No, the grip she had on him was about bone-deep fear.

It was one thing to pretend with the man who'd become so absorbed with her that he wasn't looking for inconsistencies—in her stories or in her. But to meet his family, a clan who, by his own admission, was too inquisitive, too protective? Too opinionated? They'd see right through her before the first meal was over. It wasn't that she was trying to hide something to hurt Luke because she wasn't. If he really cared about her and the past several weeks had not been mere infatuation, he'd stand by her when he found out she'd lied about a few things. Okay, yes, they were important, but so was making sure she didn't get played again. Another month or two and she'd have her answers and if he were still all-in, she'd find a way to tell him. She clutched his arm tighter, sucked in tiny breaths of cold air. Would he be happy? No, a man like Luke Donovan wouldn't want to be lied to, especially from someone he trusted. But once she explained her reasoning for keeping the truth from him, he'd understand and *that's* why the family couldn't suspect anything.

"Hey, relax." Luke smiled down at her as they stood on the front porch. "My mother's going to love you." He leaned down, kissed her temple, murmured, "Probably almost as much as I do."

I love you, he'd said when she told him about the baby. *So damn much you make my chest ache.* Oh, but he made her chest ache too, with more love than she'd ever thought possible. "Thank you," she whispered.

Luke straightened, stroked her cheek. "Anything for you, Mrs. Donovan." He opened the door, motioned for her to step inside. "Welcome to the Donovan homestead." He helped her out of her jacket, hung it on the coat tree in the corner. "There are a lot of stories floating between these walls." A sigh, a shake of his head. "That's for damn sure."

"Lucas?" A petite, older woman with dark hair approached them, her expression one of joy and excitement, her blue eyes sparkling. "Oh, Lucas, I've missed you."

"Hi, Mom." Luke made his way toward the woman and pulled her into his arms. "It's good to be home." His voice dipped, turned soft and gentle. "It's been too long."

Luke's mother eased back, sniffed. "It's so good to have you home." She turned to Helena, offered a welcoming smile. "And you've brought this beautiful young woman with you."

"Mom, meet Helena. Helena, this is my mom, Rose."

Rose Donovan didn't hesitate or hold back when she hugged Helena. "I am so very happy to meet the woman who's captured Lucas's heart." She hugged her once more, pulled away. "I knew it would happen one day." Her voice drifted, turned sad. "If only his father had lived to see it."

"Mom, I think Dad knows."

She nodded, sniffed again, and worked up a smile. "Yes, of course he does. Lucas's father always knew the goings-on in this family even when I didn't, and I suspect nothing's changed."

Luke told her his father had died, some sort of tragic accident that left them all devastated. He didn't say more other than to admit he ran from the situation and left his oldest brother to handle the fallout, an action he later regretted. Helena had run away from her life in San Diego, but she'd never regretted it. How did a person regret bad memories and a hurt so deep she didn't want to think about it? "I'm very sorry about your husband."

"Thank you, dear." Rose Donovan's gaze slid to Helena's belly. "Jonathan would be so happy to hear he's going to be a grandpa again."

"Again?" Luke asked, his expression curious.

His mother laughed. "You're not the only one with surprises. Rogan and Elizabeth are expecting, but we'll discuss that over lunch. I made a pot of chicken soup with the tiny meatballs you like. Or, if it's too early, I'll whip up a batch of buttermilk pancakes with eggs and sausage links. There's plenty of fruit, too, because I didn't know what Helena could eat or what she might like." She motioned for them to follow her to the kitchen. "Helena, do you eat meat or are you one of those vegetarians or vegans or whatever they call it?"

"I eat meat, but not a lot."

Rose slid her a look, nodded, as if to say, *I hope you're feeding my son because he likes meat—a lot of it, too.* "If you're going to be here a while, I can teach you how to make a few of Lucas's favorite recipes. He always was a good eater, but no matter how much he ate, he stayed lean like his father." Her voice slipped a notch. "Charlotte isn't so lucky. That poor girl does love her food, but if she's not careful, it ends up in places it shouldn't." She winked at Helena. "Hips, belly, behind...the usual. And then she's miserable and complaining about why calories shouldn't taste so good as she's munching on a cookie or digging into the ice cream." A raised brow and a laugh. "She's getting better, though; exercises and takes the dog for long walks, and of course it's all because of—" she gasped, cleared her throat "—all because of her new-found happiness, which you'll hear about soon enough."

Luke narrowed his gaze on his mother, rubbed his jaw. "There's a big hole in that comment and something tells me you left out the most important part."

"Maybe, but it's a surprise and she'll want to tell you yourself. Now, I want to hear all about you and Helena. How did you meet? When did you realize you were meant to be together? And the wedding?" Her eyes misted, her voice grew soft. "I do so want to hear about that. I wish I'd been there." Two blinks and a softer "I prayed it would happen and to have witnessed such a miracle?" Laughter spilled from Rose's pale lips as she swiped at her eyes. "It would have been extraordinary."

Helena darted a glance at Luke, noticed the blush on his tanned face. So, he'd really been opposed to marriage...or maybe he'd been opposed to being with one woman. The truth wasn't quite clear yet, and while he'd admitted he'd never imagined himself married with a child in the span of a few months' time, she'd thought he meant the timing was lightning speed, and not what he'd expected. Now she wasn't so sure he'd been talking about timing at all, but rather the marriage and the baby part, period. She placed a hand on her belly, rubbed the tiny bump. Would Luke regret the hasty marriage? The baby? Her? More belly rubbing, gentle, protective.

"Helena?" Luke laid a hand on her arm, his gaze settling on her belly. "Is something wrong?"

She stopped rubbing, forced a smile to hide the doubt in her heart. He mustn't see her fear. It would cloud his judgment and she had to know he wanted this life, that obligation was not the reason. Love and a desire to commit was the reason. "I'm fine. Just a little tired, I guess."

Rose Donovan shook her dark head. "Isn't it something how the fatigue hits you? One second you're mopping the floor and the next you have to sit down and close your eyes." She *tsk-tsked*. "Wait until the next one. Of course, it depends on how close together they are, but no matter the age difference, you won't be able to rest like you can with this one." A slow smile crept over her lips. "You'll see. But there's nothing like it and all the heartburn, sleepless nights, and stretch marks are worth it when you look at your child. It's a true miracle, one that should never be ignored or forgotten."

Luke cleared his throat, twice. "Mom, let's get through the first pregnancy before we start talking about the second."

"Oh... Yes, there's no rush to talk of another one or another three. You two just take your time and enjoy being together." She picked up a slice of fresh bread, handed it to Luke. "Help yourself, dear. And when you do decide to expand the family, we're all here to help, especially with the babysitting." Another smile and a pledge, "We'll do anything we can because that's what family does."

Helena tried to imagine her brother and sister offering babysitting services. It would never happen. Dominic was divorced, no kids, and Estelle had chosen two Yorkshire terriers instead of a man because she said *dogs don't break your heart.* As long as Helena delivered her work and remained within calling distance, her siblings didn't butt into her personal life. Oh, they might threaten and make a comment or two, but doing something about it because they disagreed with her? That would require an investment of time and emotion and Dominic and Estelle didn't have either to spare, at least that's what they implied whenever she called with a nonwork question. *Can't talk now...right in the middle of a meeting...gotta go...call later...* Or, *why do you feel that way? You're overreacting; can't you see that?*

They were more interested in Helena as an employee than a sister and didn't take time for her unless her personal life interfered with her work—as in a production lag. Then they were *very* interested and if the production decreased, they made a point of finding out why and who was behind the problem. The ex-fiancé was a huge issue, but Dominic said the work that resulted from the breakup was first class. Estelle agreed and encouraged her to continue writing them.

What would they say if they knew she were in love and expecting a baby? And Luke? What would they think of him? Words like *undisciplined, reckless*, and *wild* came to mind.

"Do you think you'll find out the baby's sex?" Rose Donovan glanced from her son to Helena, her blue eyes filled with such joy.

"Dunno," Luke said. "We're still talking about it." He slid a smile at Helena that pinged her heart and made her want to believe he really was all-in.

Rose sighed. "Well, your brother isn't interested in finding out if their baby is a boy or a girl. He says there aren't enough surprises left in the world and they want this to be a surprise." Another sigh, longer and more drawn out than the first. "How does he think I'm supposed to crochet baby blankets and booties if I have no idea whether the baby's a girl or a boy? He says yellow and green are fine and Elizabeth—" she slathered butter on a slice of bread and studied it "—thinks any color is suitable...maroon, gray, purple...teal...no matter the sex of the baby." She frowned, shook her head. "I don't understand the world today. In my time it was so much simpler. Pink was for girls, blue was for boys and if you didn't know, you chose green or yellow."

"Mom, do you want us to find out the sex of the baby?" Luke spoke in a gentle voice, his pale blue eyes on his mother.

Rose Donovan's face lit up with pure joy. "You would consider doing that?"

Luke glanced at Helena, then back at his mother. "We have to talk about it, but if it means that much to you—"

"We'd be happy to find out," Helena said, laying a hand on Luke's thigh. "Maybe you'd like to come with us to one of the doctor appointments?" It was the least they could do for Luke's mother who, according to him, had known her share of heartache. This was what family did, wasn't it? But Rose's next words told her not all family members were so open with their sharing.

"Bless you, children but you have made my heart sing." Rose sat back in her chair, tapped a finger against her chin. "Now if I could only find out Charlotte's intentions..."

"Charlotte?" Luke asked around a mouthful of bread. "What intentions? What did she do now?" He scooped a tiny meatball onto his spoon, plopped it in his mouth, chewed.

Luke's younger sister sounded like a hellion: full of energy and as much spunk as her brother. Two traits that weren't always understood or accepted in a female. Helena was anxious as well as hesitant to meet this sister.

"You'll see soon enough, my dear." His mother laughed, dabbed her lips with a napkin. "I can't spoil all of the surprises. Besides, if you'd thought to visit more than once a year, you might have heard the news from her yourself." She shrugged, said in a singsong voice coated with mystery, "Now you'll just have to wait to find out."

Luke sighed. "Fine. I can imagine what she's gotten into..." He turned to Helena, said in a soft voice, "My sister's got a mind of her own." He grinned, his blue eyes sparkling. "Worse than me. Headstrong, too. I pity the man who tries to tame her because that is not happening."

Rose Donovan's laughter skittered across the table, landed next to Luke and Helena. "You'd be surprised what happens when you fall in love." Her lips pulled into a wide smile. "And once you meet the man, I think you'll agree they're perfect for each other."

Chapter 4

There were too many secrets swirling around the Donovan household and Luke didn't like it. In the past, he'd usually been the one holding the secret, but to sit on the outside and try to guess what was going on? That was pure agitation and didn't sit well. He'd tried to get his mother to spill the details, like what was going on with Charlotte, who was the guy she'd fallen for, and what was all this about intentions? What intentions? His sister had never *fallen* for any guy, not that Luke knew of, but then he'd just figured it was because she'd been too mouthy and opinionated to get one to land long enough to notice the softness behind the attitude. And Rogan? That was another level of what-the-hell-is-going-on-here, especially the quickie marriage and the baby. His brother had always been a plotter and a planner. You had to be one to get excited about accounting as a profession, didn't you?

What else had happened since Luke had been gone? It's not that he wanted a play-by-play of everyone's life in this town, but this was his family; he should at least know the basics behind a new sister-in-law and a baby, shouldn't he? He stood in the backyard inspecting his mother's gardens. Snow covered the beds and branches of a few bushes. The areas would need to be rototilled in the spring; he could do that for her if she wanted. His gaze slid to the gate leading to the open area of the yard. Talk about rusty and in need of repair. Maybe he should start making a list of what needed to be fixed. It was the least he could do for his mother, and it would take some of the burden from Rogan.

He couldn't go back and undo the fact that he'd bailed on his family when they needed him, but he could show them it wouldn't happen again. That Luke Donovan was long gone, replaced with a better, more mature, sympathetic version. Was it because of Helena and the child? Of course, she made him better, made him want to be better, but the truth was that he'd gotten tired of his old lifestyle and realized it was time to grow up.

Now all he had to do was find a way to earn money. He'd been thinking about that since he and Helena decided to head to Reunion Gap. Maybe he'd talk to Rogan about a job in the factory. It wasn't his first choice, not even his fifth, but a baby cost money and he'd do whatever he had to in order to provide for his family. *His family.* Who would have ever thought he'd think about making choices for anyone but himself? Certainly not him, but here he was... If he worked in the factory he might also be able to pick up a few handyman jobs on the side. Fixing up houses—inside and outside—was something he knew about and he was pretty good at it.

Helena wanted to get a job, too, but he'd rather she concentrate on the greeting card gig and see if she could sell more cards. She'd already sold a few and if she kept at it, who knew where it would take her? Luke imagined Helena working out of the house, creating cards, and taking care of their baby.

Life was good. He and Helena were happy and had their whole future ahead of them. He turned and headed toward the house, whistling under his breath. Now all he had to do was get through tonight's dinner and the reunion with his siblings. He tried to picture it all through his wife's eyes. What would it look like? Too loud? Too bold? Too opinionated? Yup, he'd go with all of those. And too much talking, way too much talking.

But hours later as he entered the dining room with his arm around his wife's shoulders to join his mother, Rogan, Charlotte, and a woman who must be Rogan's wife, he could not have imagined the scene that became reality. And not in a good or welcome-to-the-family way. "This is my wife, Helena."

"Wife?" Rogan spat out, gaze narrowed, lips pulled into a frown. "Wife?" he repeated as if Luke had just confessed to marrying a mail-order bride.

"Your wife?" This from Charlotte whose words sputtered and landed in a heap of confusion at his feet.

Talk about making him look like a fool. Was it really that impossible to imagine him with a wife? Okay, so a wife had never been on his top 10 wish list, but he'd never expected to meet anybody like Helena. Luke squared his shoulders, stared at his brother and sister. "Right. My wife."

His mother's smile said she was happy about the announcement even if no one else was. "Yes, Lucas has brought home a wife." She clasped her hands together like she was praying, and added, "Isn't that just wonderful news?"

"Sure is. Tell us how you ended up together." Rogan paused. "Must have been love at first sight." His brother knew how to torment him with just the right amount of teasing laced with arrogance, as though he were the more intelligent one, as though he already knew what his little brother would say. Of course, the guy didn't know but he could goad Luke into spilling the truth before Luke even realized what he was doing. But not this time because the blonde sitting next to Rogan, who must be Elizabeth, clamped a hand on her husband's wrist, as if to say, *That's enough. Please don't torment your brother.*

Luke shifted from one foot to the other, cleared his throat. If he admitted that it pretty much *was* love at first sight, he'd sound like a fool and his siblings wouldn't believe him anyway. He did not want to look like an idiot in front of Helena or like the guy he'd been...the one who couldn't commit and wouldn't consider a wife, let alone a child.

Luke opened his mouth to spit out the news and prepare for the back-lash when—

"It *was* love at first sight," his wife blurted out. "A few days after we met we were inseparable and realized we never wanted to be apart." She clung to his arm, squeezed tight. "It was destiny."

"Destiny." Rogan mouthed the word as though he didn't under-stand its meaning.

Charlotte pushed back her chair and made her way to the other side of the table, opening her arms to her new sister-in-law. "Congrat-ulations." She hugged Helena, then turned to Luke. "Wow. Destiny led you to each other… How wonderful." His sister hugged him tight, leaned on tiptoe and whispered in his ear. "Are you crazy?" Her smile stayed in place until she was back in her seat and only then did it slip an inch. If you weren't watching for it, you'd never have noticed.

Happy homecoming. This was life at the Donovans'. A place where no one kept their thoughts to themselves and everyone had an opinion and felt it was their right and duty to share it. Luke forced a tight smile, pulled out a chair for Helena, and sank into the one beside her. "I'm hungry," he said, eyeing the roasted potatoes and fried chicken. "It's been a long time since I've had Mom's fried chicken." His siblings did have the courtesy to wait until he'd loaded up his plate and taken a few bites before they started on him again. This time it was Charlotte who conducted the interrogation, but he knew Rogan would tag-team and neither would stop until they had answers. Helena said she had a brother and sister, but he bet they weren't loudmouth, opinionated siblings like these two.

"So, what's been going on in your world?" Charlotte forked a bite of potato, pointed it at him. "Fill us in on the last several months since you've been pretty much invisible." She eyed him, her green eyes filling with humor and curiosity. "You spill and then I will, too. We'll compare notes and see who's got the bigger surprise."

Luke didn't miss the disgusted sigh from his brother or the soft laugh from his new sister-in-law. Charlotte had a bigger surprise than a new spouse and a baby on the way? Doubtful, but he'd like to hear it because it probably had to do with the guy his mother told him about. This was not how he'd wanted to tell his siblings he was going to be a father. He'd planned to work up to it, show them how different he was from the last time they'd seen him, but it wasn't going to play out that way. "Okay, I'm game." He tore a roll in half, slathered it with butter. "Helena's pregnant." Yeah, nobody but his mother had expected that one. Luke eyed his siblings, slid them a smile. "Didn't see that one coming, did you?"

It was Helena's turn to clasp his hand and squeeze. "It was a bit of a surprise," she said, her words landing in the middle of the table with a thud. She did her best to recover as she rushed on, "We're very excited about the baby...and...everything."

"Huh." This from Charlotte who homed in on Luke as if trying to determine the accuracy of his new wife's comments. "Well, you've got me beat. My surprise isn't nearly as earth-shattering as a baby announcement."

Rogan shook his head, smiled at Charlotte. "I'm not so sure Luke will agree on that one. In fact, I seem to remember a particular animosity toward your husband and I doubt his feelings have changed much."

"Husband?" Charlotte was married? The rest of Rogan's words flitted through his brain, skidded to a halt. "Animosity?" He darted a glance from his brother to his sister. "There's only one guy I can't stand, and—"

The front door opened and a voice that sounded an awful lot like the jerk who annoyed the crap out of Luke called out, "Honey, we're home!"

"Tate Alexander?" Luke stared at his sister. "This is a joke, right?" He couldn't stand the guy and his too-good looks, his fancy words, and fancier cars.

Charlotte pushed back her chair, stood, and made her way to the other side of the table, closer to the voice they'd just heard. "Tate and I got married last month."

"You and Alexander. Married." Luke rubbed his forehead, tried to make sense of what his sister had just told him. Tate Alexander was an arrogant piece of crap who'd been born with money and entitlement and no way was he going to touch Luke's little sister—except apparently, he already had. "Where is he?" Luke balled his fists, scowled. Before he could continue his rant about his sister's new husband, a golden retriever bounded into the dining room and jumped on him, mouth open, tail wagging.

"Winston! Down!" Charlotte rushed to the dog, lifted a finger, and repeated, "Down." The dog settled at her feet, tail still wagging.

"This your mutt?" Luke asked.

She nodded. "He doesn't like to be called a mutt. His name's Winston."

The other mutt in her life stepped into the room, brushed a hand along Charlotte's cheek and kissed her, murmuring in her ear. Then he turned to Luke and said, "Welcome back to Reunion Gap." He held out a hand and left Luke no choice but to shake it or risk looking like an idiot. That was the pain-in-the-ass annoyance about Alexander: he always had the upper hand and knew how to play it to make you look like a fool.

"We're going to have a talk," Luke said, gaze narrowed, breathing harsh. "My brother might have given you his blessing to marry our sister, but I sure as hell didn't."

"Hey, hey, cool it, Luke." Rogan shot him a look. "Charlotte's a big girl and this guy's not as big a pain as he used to be." He shrugged, added, "Besides, he bought her a dog and he's building her a house and she's a whole lot calmer now that he's in the picture."

Charlotte made a face at Rogan. "Can you not see that I'm standing right here? And I was never not calm." She eyed her new husband. "Was I grouchy and wired before we got together?"

The guy's expression softened, and his voice slipped three octaves. "Maybe a little?"

Okay, with an answer like that it was obvious the guy loved Charlotte. Nobody would be that nice to his sister and her bitchiness unless he really loved her and could overlook it. Or unless his presence made her less bitchy. "So, you and Tate Alexander..."

Charlotte clutched her husband's arm, leaned on tiptoe and kissed him. "Yup, me and Tate Alexander." She sighed and turned to Rogan. "You forgot to tell Luke what else Tate did."

"Married you and didn't tell me about it?"

"No, and that was my idea, so stop blaming him." Her voice turned all soft and gooey. "He made me the happiest woman in the world."

Gag. Now she sounded like one of those Annabelle Grace greeting cards he'd seen when he picked up a card for Helena. Was it necessary to spill your guts and other organs to prove you cared about a person? Who wrote those things anyway? Helena's would be sweet not nauseating, and one of these days she'd share one with him. And if they were really lucky, one of these days she'd sell some because they could use the cash.

"Tate, dear, have a seat and fix yourself a plate." Rose Donovan smiled at the guy, her cheeks bursting with color, voice soft as melted butter on biscuits. "I know how much you like my fried chicken."

Alexander's silver eyes sparkled. "One of my favorite dishes, Rose." He patted his flat belly, smiled. "I've been thinking about this all day." He paused, and the smile stretched across his face. "And the blueberry coffee cake I thought I smelled this morning."

He thought he smelled blueberry coffee cake this morning? How could that be? Was the guy staying here? Impossible. Tate Alexander lived in mansions, not run-down houses with questionable heating systems and low-end appliances. And how did the guy know about his mother's famous fried chicken unless he'd sampled it a time or two? Luke sucked in a breath, forced his voice to remain calm as he shot a glance at Charlotte's husband. "What were you doing here this morning?"

The guy didn't have time to respond because Charlotte stepped in. "We live here." Pause, and then, "Until our house is built."

"Really?" Luke rubbed his jaw, narrowed his gaze on the man

who'd annoyed him since he'd seen him driving around town in a new sporty Mercedes. "Well, isn't that interesting? Why can't you live in your mansion or rent out a block? Or travel to the next city? Why can't you live anywhere but here?"

The man's face turned three shades of red. "I..." More red bursting on that too-perfect face, smothering his good looks.

"Stop it, Luke," Charlotte spat out, like she was going to protect the guy. "Can't you see this is an uncomfortable situation for him? Do you think maybe he doesn't want to talk about it?" Her lips thinned, those green eyes burned into him. "No, of course not, because you still think it's only about you. Well, it's not. Other people get hurt, too, and you'd better take a crash course in sensitivity or you're going to be spending a lot of nights on the couch."

"Hey, what did I do?" What the hell had just happened? Rogan shook his head, turned back to his plate, muttering something about family. "Will somebody tell me what I did?" Luke set down his fork, looked around the table. "Somebody? Anybody?"

He did not expect Helena to be the one to speak up and the fact that she did made him wish he'd kept his mouth shut and just shook the damn guy's hand. Period.

"You embarrassed your brother-in-law," she said. "It's obvious there's a reason he's not living in a family residence or somewhere else." Her voice gentled as she met Tate Alexander's guarded stare. "Whatever the reason, it's private and should be respected."

Now Helena was sticking up for the guy? "I just asked a question and in this family, that's what we do." He scowled at his sister's husband. "No sugarcoating, no worrying about bruising an ego or tiptoeing around feelings. If the rules of engagement have changed, then let me know."

"Why do you have to be like that?" Charlotte glared at him, clutched her husband's arm.

"He didn't mean anything by it." This from the injured party himself spoken in a low voice stuffed with culture and class. "We're staying here because I've had a falling-out with my father. Part business—" he glanced at Charlotte "—mostly personal. We could move in with Camille, but her situation is tenuous and... Honestly, this place makes me feel like I belong to a family. I've never known that before and I didn't want to give it up."

"Nor should you," Rose Donovan said from her place at the head of the table. "We can all coexist." She shot a sharp glance at Luke. "Tate defended your sister against his father, if you must know, and that's what caused the falling-out."

Talk about feeling like a jerk. Luke cleared his throat. "Guess I overreacted."

"Again," Rogan mumbled, loud enough for Luke to hear him. And then, "So, Helena, this is what dinner at the Donovans' looks like. Aren't you glad you joined the family?"

Chapter 5

"So, what do you think of Helena?"

When Charlotte asked questions like that, it meant she'd already done her analysis and wanted to see if he agreed. Of course, Tate's bride wouldn't come right out and admit it or offer up her thoughts. She preferred to test him and while he'd like to believe they were at a point in their relationship where she could trust him to tell her the truth, it wasn't about that at all. Charlotte enjoyed the cerebral challenge and the occasional sparring that came with their discussions, especially when they didn't agree.

And because they were still living in Rose Donovan's house and sleeping in Charlotte's old room with the paper-thin walls, most of their discussions took place at night. In the dark. Naked. Who could argue with that? In fact, who cared about arguing at all when there was a naked woman snuggling against him, all warm and cozy, her curious fingers exploring his body?

If only she would learn that controversial discussions belonged in a neutral location with clothes on and bodies not touching—like a coffee shop or a restaurant. Hell, he'd even agree to his office if it meant keeping possible disagreements out of the bedroom. But no. When his wife was ready to talk, she was ready, and no amount of coaxing or soft persuasion would get her to stall until morning. Tate let out a long sigh, sifted her hair through his fingers.

"Why the sigh?"

She lifted her head, squinted at him in the semi-darkness. At least there was a nightlight to illuminate a path to the door. There hadn't been one when he'd first moved in and he'd tripped over Charlotte's discarded items—shoes, jeans, a handbag—since she didn't believe in drawers *or* a closet. When he'd landed on the floor in pitch blackness, he let out a string of curses that woke Rose. That's when the nightlight appeared. It would have made more sense for Charlotte to pick up the trail she left on the floor, but logic and his wife didn't always see eye to eye. "I was just thinking that when we move into the new house, you're going to have two walk-in closets and I bet you won't use either of them."

It was her turn to sigh. "Probably not, but if you start harping on me, you'll be sleeping in there."

He chuckled. If he were sleeping in the closet, she'd be right beside him and she knew it. Didn't she tell him every night that she loved sleeping next to him, loved the sound of his breathing, the feel of his skin against hers? But if she wanted to believe she'd boot him to the closet, fine, let her believe it. "Right."

She leaned up, nibbled his ear. "I am such a liar, aren't I?"

Tate smiled into the darkness. "Yup." More nibbling followed by a stroke of her tongue along his neck. Tate sucked in a breath. "If you want to talk about your new sister-in-law, you better put that tongue on pause or we won't be talking until tomorrow."

Charlotte lifted her head. "I was only—"

"Distracting me?" he said in a low voice. "Driving me wild? Making me forget what little brain capacity I have left when you're around?"

"Keep talking."

She definitely liked to hear about the power and the control she had over him, but it was no different for her, which was why they were a perfect match. If he got his thoughts out fast, they could pick up where they left off with more touching and a lot more stroking. "I thought she was nice."

"She did seem nice enough. Pretty. A bit shy. Nothing like I would ever imagine Luke being attracted to and certainly not someone he'd marry." Charlotte's tone shifted with suspicion. "Don't forget that she's pregnant. A pregnancy always factors in when there's a hasty wedding."

He worked up a smile, tucked a lock of hair behind her ear. "So, if I'd gotten you pregnant, would we have run to the altar and saved ourselves a lot of grief?"

He didn't miss the double huff. "Not necessarily. The problems would have been there whether we were married or not, and that's what I'm wondering about those two. They've only known each other a few months and there's no way she doesn't have a history or a past. Doesn't it make you wonder how she ended up with someone like Luke?" Big sigh. "I love my brother, but he was never marriage material. Heck, he wasn't even boyfriend material and he didn't want to be. Luke was the kind of guy who could create an explosion just by looking at you, but he wasn't the staying kind." She stroked his cheek, her voice soft. "Kind of like you."

Like him? Was she serious? He was nothing like Luke Donovan: not the style, the delivery, or the sentiment. From the stories Tate had heard, when Donovan was through with a woman, he was through. No sweet send-off, no gifts, nothing but unreturned phone calls. How could Charlotte think he and her brother had *anything* in common? It was an insult and if he were the type to let his feelings get hurt, then he'd have to admit that hearing his wife make comparisons like that *did* hurt his feelings. "Your brother and I are nothing alike."

Charlotte inched closer to place the softest kiss on his lips. "You're not like that anymore. And I know you're always kind and considerate and you're not heartless or cruel, but you did break a lot of hearts and that's what I meant." Another kiss, this one deeper.

"Maybe your brother's a changed man," Tate murmured against

her lips. "Maybe this one's made him a better man… Like you made me. Worthy, committed, husband material."

"Maybe. But there's something about her that doesn't feel right. People only see the harsh side of Luke but he's not that way. He's sensitive and he does care but he's afraid to show it. If he really loves her, I want to make sure she loves him, too, and didn't just marry him because they're going to have a baby. Do you know how terrible it would be if he gave his heart to somebody who didn't feel the same way? Somebody who wasn't committed to him like he was to her?"

Oh, yes, he knew all about it because that had been his life before Charlotte admitted she loved him. The pain of the memory still lived in his heart, still tormented his soul now and again. "Trust me, I know all about it."

"I love you, Tate Alexander, and I'm never going to hurt you like that again. We just have to make sure Luke's wife isn't going to hurt him either."

CARTER ALEXANDER POSSESSED book intelligence and charm with a way about him that told a woman he knew what he wanted and wasn't afraid to go after it—no matter the cost or the inconvenience. While that might be true in varying degrees, it was also true that when he created a mess—and he *always* created a mess—Harrison was the one he called to clean it up. There was always a sad story, always a reason another person was to blame, and there was always a woman involved. Why couldn't Carter be satisfied with Camille? The woman was too damn smart for him, too clever, too intelligent.

And now she planned to divorce him.

Harrison could see where news that her husband had gotten his current girlfriend pregnant might cause concern and perhaps in a moment of haste and emotion, elicit divorce papers. But Alexanders did *not* get divorces, and Harrison refused to sit by and watch Carter and Camille become the first casualties. It wasn't that he necessarily believed in the sanctity of marriage because he'd broken his vows more than once; it was the Alexander name that must remain stronger and mightier than any other in the area. Divorce would weaken it and that possibility was unacceptable.

He'd summoned his brother this afternoon to discuss the matter of Carter's pregnant girlfriend. No doubt, Harrison would have to step in again and take care of things just as he'd done before. This time, however, Carter would not slink away unscathed with nothing more than a feeble promise to *make better choices*. No, this time his younger brother would feel the pain and repercussions of his actions and if they were deep and harsh enough, Carter might finally learn his lesson.

Or not.

The sharp rap on the library door came seconds before Carter entered with a "Thanks for taking the time to see me."

Harrison stood, eyed the man who'd bedded enough women to fill a movie theater and for a few seconds, had loved them all. Only a fool would admit to such nonsense or a person who wanted to excuse his behavior and bury all manner of guilt. "You look terrible. Were you up all night worrying about this meeting or have you finally realized you're about to lose the best thing that ever happened to you?"

Carter shrugged, shook Harrison's hand, and slid onto the couch. "It's a damn mess and I'll be glad when it's over." He rifled a hand through his perfect hair, frowned. "She really thinks she's got the upper hand this time. Like she can tell me what to do and I'm going to listen." Laughter spilled from his full lips. "Those days are over, and I can't wait to be rid of her."

There was no need to identify the *she* in the conversation because they both knew he was referring to his wife, the woman he'd married to defy the Alexander-Donovan feud. For a man who'd never known struggle or disappointment, he was bound to fail sooner or later, and when the fail came, it would be monumental. "I heard about your pregnant girlfriend. How old is she? Twenty-one? Twenty-two?"

Swirls of pink crept up Carter's neck, colored his tanned cheeks. "Twenty-three next month."

"Ah, twenty-three." Harrison poured them both a whiskey, handed a glass to his brother and said, "Drink up, you're going to need it." The pink on his brother's face inched to his ears, deepened.

"Look, I know what you're going to say but I deserve to be happy and I'm not going to miss out."

Harrison should never have helped him the first time he got a girl in trouble. He should have forced Carter to face the consequences of his recklessness. Maybe his brother thought those dimples would get him out of a paternity suit and child support until the kid was eighteen, but most judges didn't think that way; the one in Reunion Gap certainly didn't.

But Carter had still been in college with the whole world ahead of him and while he'd deserved to clean up his own mess, Harrison had stepped in and taken care of it. *Just this once,* he'd told his brother. *I'm not going to do it again, so you better think before you unzip your pants.* But it hadn't been just once. There'd been other times, other problems, and Harrison had always taken care of it. His father said that's what family did, and his mother had agreed. It was his mother who begged him to save his little brother. *A child will ruin his whole life. You can't let this happen. You have to help him. Please. Please. You can make things right, Harrison.* Her requests continued over the years, each time killing another piece of the goodness that still lived in him until his father snuffed out the last shreds of decency with his final words. *You must do whatever is necessary to protect our family. Do you understand? Whatever is necessary.* One last breath that ended with *That's what families do.*

Years and too many regrets later, he'd learned that families did not compromise themselves or their principles, families cared about one another, *loved* one another. Of course, the realization was too stark, too impossible to acknowledge or accept. The only choice Harrison had was to fight it and bury the truths so deep in his soul he'd never find them.

46

And that's exactly what he did.

Now he'd been left with another problem that was no different from the first one his brother created too many years ago. But this time the outcome would be different because Carter would learn the pain of his actions. Harrison sipped his whiskey, said in a quiet voice, "Tell me about your plans." Gathering information and determining the other person's agenda before offering a solution was a solid strategy. It provided an edge and Harrison knew all about leveraging to his advantage.

Carter shrugged. "We haven't really talked about it. Get the divorce first, have the baby, find a place to live." He eyed Harrison, worked up a smile. "There's a lot on the outside of town not far from where Tate's planning to build. I'm thinking about buying it. Only problem is, I'm a little short on cash and with the divorce, it's not looking like I'm going to have much capital before the settlement. I was hoping you might give me a loan." Pause, a deeper smile, this one pulling out those damnable dimples his brother favored. "Just until the settlement goes through, then I'll pay you back."

Of course, Carter wanted a loan and of course he thought Harrison would give him one. Why wouldn't he when he'd bailed his brother out for years? The man still owed him for the last two loans he'd given him. There'd be no mention of that because Carter probably didn't even remember. No, his only concern was his latest predicament. "You're looking at a lot near Tate." His son had married the Donovan girl and now he planned to build her a house and live happily ever after. They'd have a few children and he heard there was even a dog. Tate thought he loved her and maybe he did, but was that really the point? Love could only take a person so far. It was breeding and manners that mattered.

But even as he thought this, he knew his objection to Charlotte Donovan had nothing to do with breeding or manners. No, it was so much deeper than that. Charlotte Donovan reminded him of her mother and *that* was the real issue. He could not look at Rose's daughter without remembering what he and her mother had shared or the man who'd stolen that happiness. Rose might be angry with Harrison and had even threatened him, but they were only words. She would never harm him and one day she'd realize why. That's when she would have to admit she still cared about him, had always cared. But that would come later because right now he had a wayward brother to deal with and a relationship to end.

"I can't help you, Carter. You made this mess and you're going to have to clean it up."

"I didn't really make this mess on my own; it just sort of happened." He made a sour face like he used to when he was a boy and got caught wearing their father's aftershave. The denials had been strong back then, too, even though he'd drenched himself in the stuff. "It all just landed on me and before I knew it, she was pregnant, and I was getting handed divorce papers… I didn't really want that but nobody's going to tell me what to do. She doesn't own me."

"She, as in your wife or your girlfriend? Or maybe you're talking about both?" There were days when Harrison grew tired of the constant battles and the stupidity of others. Why did everyone always think he would clean up their messes no matter how much stench they caused? When he'd been laid up with the recent illness—he still refused to call it a stroke—nobody had bothered him unless it was a request to move a body part or practice his speech. There'd been a small amount of peace in that but if he were honest, he'd admit he wanted to be in the middle of decisions, even if they'd been pulled from a cesspool. It was all about control and he was a man who thrived on it.

Carter polished off his whiskey, clutched the empty glass in is hand. "I'm talking about Camille."

"Your wife."

His brother ignored the jab, frowned. "If she hadn't stirred up the whole town with her woe-is-me story, my practice wouldn't be suffering. But it is, and it's put me in a bind. I need your help, Harrison." Pause. "One last time."

Carter meant one last time until the next time. Harrison ignored his brother's begging, circled back to the mention of his practice. "Maybe people don't want a doctor removing their moles when they aren't sure what else is happening on the exam table." His source had told him about the escapades in Carter's office with the girlfriend. There'd been others, too: the receptionist, the medical supply salesperson, the sister of one of his patients. Harrison had never been a saint, but at least he had used discretion.

Carter rolled up the sleeves of one of the designer shirts he loved so much, wiped a hand over his brow. "Maybe I've made a few bad choices, but I've learned from them. Things will be different, you'll see. I just need a little time and capital."

The more his brother talked, the more desperate he became, like the bird trapped in the blueberry netting when Harrison was a child. His mother had insisted the netting cover all the blueberry bushes and when the little bird got caught, she wanted him to dispose of it. *He's done enough destruction*, she claimed. *Get rid of him. He's breathed enough air on this earth. He offers no value.* He caught the bird but ignored his mother's demand and tried to untangle it from the netting. The bird's tiny feet twisted in the netting and when Harrison finally freed the animal, it limped away in a sad testimony to freedom. *He'll be someone's dinner tonight*, his mother had said. *You would have been better off putting him out of his misery. Think about that next time you want to show mercy.* He wondered about the bird for years after, still thought about it some days, usually right before he went after his next target. Would life have been different if he'd had parents who possessed an ounce of compassion? Or was cruelty inbred in his soul? "I'll help you get your practice back to full capacity; I'll even tell you how to do it."

His brother sat up, anxious, eager, not unlike the bird caught in the netting. "You will? Just tell me what to do Harrison. Anything."

"Get rid of the girl. There will be no divorce."

Chapter 6

I f almost thirty years of marriage had taught Camille Alexander
one lesson, it was that no matter how much you wanted it,
divorce was an ugly animal. It was one thing to live with the
failings and annoyances of another person, to make side deals with
your conscience that said you'd look the other way when you smelled
another woman's perfume on his shirt or when he arrived home after
you'd gone to bed... You could even tell yourself you didn't care that
he no longer looked at you with longing or vague interest, and you
could do it all because you'd made a deal. But the deal wasn't with
him because you'd realized long ago there wasn't a damn thing you
could do to change his ways or his disinterest in you and the marriage.

No, the deal you'd made was with yourself. How much could you
take, for how long, and to what degree? Of course, you always started
out vowing not to settle for *anything*, and yet, when faced with the
reality of a less-than-ideal marriage, two small children, and a mountain of broken dreams, did you just walk out? Could you? That's when
you negotiated with yourself and changed your expectations. Maybe
that's when you stopped believing in happily-ever-after or even
happy-for-now and settled for surviving-and-still-breathing.

And as the years and betrayals increased, so did what you were willing to ignore until you didn't recognize who you'd become. Camille could blame Carter for his cheating ways, his glib tongue, his self-absorption, but she was the one who'd permitted it, accepted it, and changed because of it.

What did that say about her? Years ago, her brother had taken her aside and in the soft-spoken, nonjudgmental manner that made Jonathan Donovan one of the most respected people in the community, he'd tried to guide her. *There's been talk, Cammie...about Carter. It's not good...it involves other women.* He hadn't said another woman because that would have been a misstatement and her brother was not given to those. *You always had such dreams... If you need my help, I'm here.* She'd been unable to do more than nod because once she spoke the words, they would be too real. Her brother hugged her, offered his help once more, and never again spoke of Carter's affairs.

What might have happened if she'd asked for that help? Would she have found the strength to leave Carter? File for divorce? Raise the children and start over? She'd clung to her marriage and the life she enjoyed because of it and refused to acknowledge both were built on lies.

Now, all these years later, Carter was no different than he'd always been. Still too handsome, too arrogant, too self-absorbed with a young girlfriend...a *pregnant* young girlfriend. Camille sighed, rubbed her temples. Who was she kidding? Should she pretend surprise or shock? Mindy, the sex toy, was probably *not* the first young, pregnant girlfriend but Camille did not want to know. At some point a person had to shut down the past and refuse to scratch open more wounds that would bleed details and only make the hate stronger.

None of it mattered. Camille was not the person she'd been, the one who would not give up a bad marriage because of the children, the status, the money, her right to remain married. She'd done all of that and to what end? The children hadn't even come home for Christmas, thanks to their father's meddling. What did that say about them?

Simon and Victoria hadn't been interested in finding out any details behind their father's comments that their *Mother was on a rampage and had kicked him out of the house.* Indeed. No child wants to be plunked in the middle of a divorce, no matter their age, but could they not have been a tad concerned for their mother's welfare?

Apparently not. They hadn't even asked about their gifts. Camille massaged her right temple harder. Life was not going to get better until she stopped feeling sorry for herself and the disappointments that stymied her. Booting her husband from the house and filing for divorce were the first steps in a long journey, but if she were going to have a second chance at happiness and a decent life, she'd have to find a way to remain upbeat, to persevere, no matter what.

And it was time to let her children accept their actions along with the accompanying consequences. No more obsessive parenting or trying to remove every negative outcome from their existence. Reality held a multitude of disappointments, and Camille was done inserting false hopes and reworked agendas so that Simon and Victoria would never know a second of defeat.

It was time to take care of herself, grow stronger, more resilient, more alive, and she was going to do it.

No matter what.

The self-help and renewal mantra spiraled through her and took shape in the form of daily journal writing, exercise, meditation, reading, and she'd even signed up for a ballroom dance class. Imagine that? She didn't tell anyone, not even Rose, the queen of ballroom dancing, because this was private and something she planned to do just for herself. Camille had even signed up two towns away so Reunion Gap residents wouldn't recognize the estranged wife of philanderer Dr. Carter Alexander.

Yes, it had come to that. In the past she'd held her head high and if anyone were bold enough to stare at her a second too long, she'd skewer them with a look. But once she'd acknowledged the cold and bitter truth that her husband would *never* change no matter what she did, the fight to pretend she controlled her marriage *and* her husband ended. Now it was a matter of getting through the divorce and figuring out what to do with the rest of her life.

Staying busy was key and putting in hours at Nicki's boutique helped. Plus, Camille had her own confidante and cheerleader in Nicki Price. The woman was young and vibrant, with two small children and a husband who adored her. Nicki knew about love and commitment and wanted to give back to the town that had welcomed her one lonely Christmas and changed her life. *You're a big part of this town*, she'd told Camille. *I'll always be here for you.*

Camille removed a red dress from a box filled with designer clothes, smoothed the Peter Pan collar, and slid a glance at Nicki. "My nephew brought home a wife… A pregnant one."

Her friend stared at her. "Luke? The one you told me would never settle down?"

"Yes, *that* one. Rose said the girl's a real looker: dark-haired, eyes the color of amber, quiet, with the nicest manners." She shrugged, narrowed her gaze on the gold buttons stitched along the front of the dress. "I can see how he'd be attracted by the good looks, but the quiet and the manners? That doesn't sound like Luke's type, but who knows? Maybe she's changed him, or maybe news that he's going to be a father has..." Dear Lord, she hoped the girl hadn't trapped her nephew.

"You'll get a better feel when you meet her."

"Right, but Rose is a pretty good judge of her children's significant others. She hit it right on with Tate and she loved Elizabeth, though it took a while for her children to see the merits of their future spouses. Not Rose." A smile flitted over her lips. "Rose always knew. She seems to like Luke's wife but says she doesn't know much about her. Name's Helena. Classy, don't you think?"

"Helena," Nicki repeated. "Yes, very classy. So, give me the details. Where's she from, what does she do, how does she act toward Luke?"

"The real question seems to be what happened to my nephew? I hear Luke's waist-deep crazy about her and not afraid to show it. *That* was never his style. He's what they used to call *besotted* back in the day. Can't see anyone or anything but his wife. Rose says there's something about the girl she can't quite figure out: a sophistication that goes beyond the name and the manners. I can't wait to meet her and draw my own conclusions." She let out a soft laugh. "I do love puzzles and investigating. I think I missed my calling." Hadn't the private investigator who'd visited Reunion Gap said she had good intuition and an inquisitive nature? Yes, Lester Conroy had told her that and she should have pressed him for details on how to turn those traits into a profession. She missed the lanky former Texan and had thought about contacting him a time or two. Maybe she still would...see what he had to say about her pursuing an investigative career.

"But what about Helena?"

Yes, what about Helena? "Rose said she was waitressing in a Chinese restaurant somewhere outside of Denver. Luke had a bad cold and went in search of hot-and-sour soup and found Helena. Next thing you know she's pregnant and they're getting married." There were a lot of holes in that short story and Camille was going to find every one of them. Family protected family, and no one was going to hurt her nephew. Luke Donovan might think he was big and tough and he was, but she'd bet her diamond bracelet he didn't know about a broken heart—unless he was the one doing the breaking.

"Well." Nicki picked up a lint roller, eased it over a pair of black slacks. "Sounds a bit...quick."

"Hmm. I'd say." Camille pushed the dress aside, grabbed a pad of paper and pen, and began making notes. An investigator must be prepared.

"Camille?" Nicki leaned toward her, glanced at the notepad. "Name of restaurant? Town in Colorado? Length of stay? Mutual friends? Hometown?" She scrunched her nose, frowned. "What are you doing?"

"I'm getting ready to meet Luke's wife," she said with a sly smile. "How am I going to find out the truth if I don't know the right questions to ask?"

Two days later, Camille strutted into the Donovans' carrying a container of Luke's favorite chocolate oatmeal cookies and a six-pack of craft beer. The boy had always been partial to heavy ale and, according to Tate, this was a winner.

Rose took her coat and motioned toward the back of the house. "They're in the sunroom looking at baby pictures of Luke."

"Ah." Camille leaned close to Rose, whispered, "What have you done with my nephew and who's the impostor in his place?" The Luke she remembered didn't like to have his photo taken, and if he were forced, he made everyone miserable until they gave up.

"Interesting, isn't it?" Rose shrugged, her lips pulling into a gentle smile. "My boy's in love and it's a miracle to watch. I've never seen him kinder or more caring than when he's around Helena." She laid a hand on her heart, blinked hard. "I just want him to be happy and I pray she's everything he thinks she is."

Camille laid a hand on Rose's arm, worked up a smile. "That's why I'm here, Rose." Her voice shifted to a no-nonsense tone. "To make sure she's exactly who she says she is. Don't you worry; we'll find out."

"But what if she's not?" Rose's eyes filled with tears, her voice wobbled. "What then?"

Worries like this sent Rose into a tailspin and a downward spiral. It had happened after Jonathan's disastrous money losses and again with his tragic death. She'd been unable to pull herself out of the sadness and misery that had suffocated her, and while medication and doctors helped, they were not a cure. Camille would not have Rose's mental state on her conscience. "Let me handle this. I promise to find out and report back to you."

An hour later, Camille determined that Rose had not misread or underestimated her son and his wife's affection for each other. The couple was in love, no doubt about it, but that wasn't what Camille wanted to ascertain. No, she needed the background information on the newest Donovan addition so she could determine the woman's intentions. Unfortunately, with Luke within touching distance of his wife, it wasn't going to happen. The boy seemed overprotective and determined to shield Helena from too many questions. Inquiring was the Donovan way and he knew that, which was most likely why he'd opted to answer most of the questions—even the ones directed at his wife. After he'd intercepted the first few inquiries, Helena sat very still, shoulders squared, expression unreadable though she did offer smiles when appropriate. But the darn smiles did not reach her eyes or spread to the rest of her face, a clear indication that Helena was not pleased with her husband's interference. The behavior also revealed something else, something far more important: class and style.

Luke may not have recognized them for what they were—signs of a privileged life—but for a woman who'd spent too many years emulating them, Camille spotted them. Helena was hiding a life she didn't want Luke to know about.

The only question that mattered now was why.

The opportunity to study Helena Donovan and gather information without intrusion came the next day when Camille invited her for coffee at her home. Actually, coffee was off the list because according to Rose, Luke and Helena wanted only healthy choices for their child. Good for them. Healthy choices. Safe choices. It was an admirable goal and yet quite unattainable once the child left the womb. Parents could grow organic food, encourage intellectual stimulation, and promote an active lifestyle, but they could not keep them safe from bad choices, accidents, or the wrong partner. "So, you plan to make your own baby food? Interesting concept."

Helena nodded, her amber eyes bright with enthusiasm. "I've read up on making baby food and it looks so easy. You can even freeze the food in small containers." She sipped her water, nodded again. "Peas, green beans, sweet potatoes. Luke said he saw something about baby smoothies you can make, and he wants us to try it out."

"Luke said that?" Camille raised a brow. That did not sound at all like her nephew. The boy had never been interested in healthy choices, a healthy lifestyle, or healthy anything. Big, bold, risky, stuffed with flavor had been what interested him. His father had caught him smoking at sixteen, drinking, too...and the girls? She did not want to remember the times she'd listened to Jonathan worry about his second son or the poor choices he was making that would no doubt make him a father.

And now it had happened, and while he was older and—hopefully—more mature than he'd been as a teenager, this was still Luke they were talking about—the reckless Donovan who'd once vowed never to be tied to one woman. Hmm. But he'd tied himself to this delicate flower by giving her a ring and a baby in her belly. Camille sipped her coffee, studied the young woman. The fresh complexion, pale lips, and dark hair were a refreshing change from Luke's usual painted and dyed companions. But the absence of a tight sweater and the bosom size to go with it was very interesting.

Camille would like to believe that her nephew had grown up and selected a partner whose heart and intentions were as wholesome as her physical appearance. But looks didn't always tell the true story and who knew that better than Camille? She'd pretended around her relationship with her husband most of her marriage, and she owed it to Luke to find out why his new wife hadn't told him what Camille suspected: Helena had known wealth and privilege. The subtle airs, the casual grace, the unmistakable manners were indicators of a past life and intuition told Camille there was more the woman hadn't told her husband.

And that's what Camille intended to find out.

"Tell me again about your family? I know people in San Diego and I've visited several times. Lovely city." Had the girl flinched just now? Ah, Camille believed she had. Now why was that?

"I have an older brother and sister." Pause, a lick of her full lips followed by "My parents died when I was young."

What did *that* mean? "I'm so sorry. How old were you?" Helena's hesitation filled the room. She didn't want to answer the question, which meant there was valuable information tucked away just waiting to be unearthed by the right listener.

Luke's wife cleared her throat twice, said in a voice that sounded like she was reciting from a book, "I was eleven when Dad died; sixteen with my mother."

Oh, how Camille wanted to poke around for details but not even an inquisitive person like herself would be so brazen. At least not yet. The key would be to gain the girl's trust and then begin peeling away the layers of her past to locate significant gaps and a timeline. Her private investigator friend, Lester Conroy, told her a soft touch got a lot more solved than a rough hand. Lester would know since he'd brokered Jennifer Merrick's reunion with her mother, no small feat after a ten-year estrangement. "How tragic. Luke's father died a few years back and it was very difficult on everyone." Especially since they didn't know if the fall was an accident or intentional.

"Yes, he told me it was a horrible accident."

An accident? Perhaps it was easier to rewrite a painful experience to make it more manageable and that's certainly what they'd all done. But it didn't make it true. Maybe Jonathan's death was an accident, but probably not. "Horrible, indeed." Camille set down her coffee cup, leaned toward Helena, and let emotion drip out. "We'll be your family, dear, don't you worry. There are enough Donovans and Alexanders to form a small community." She sniffed, added, "Not all the Alexanders, though. I'll have to remove my brother-in-law, Harrison, and my soon-to-be-ex-husband, Carter, from the list."

Red tinged the girl's cheeks. "I'm sorry about your..."

"Estranged husband?" Camille shrugged, pursed her lips. "It's long overdue." She'd practiced those words for weeks, but she finally believed them. Divorcing Carter was indeed long overdue, and she'd be glad when she could dissociate herself from him and his pregnant girlfriend. "Sometimes people aren't who we think they are, or we tend to make them into what we want to believe they are. I know because that's what I did." Her gaze drifted to Helena's, held it. "But over time the truth leaks out, creating chaos and destruction in our lives, making us question the past, the present, even the future. Did he love me? Does he love me? Heavens, does he love *her*?" Camille's voice slipped to a whisper. "It makes us question ourselves." Pause. "Don't ever let that happen to you because it's horrible and demeaning."

"You're a strong woman..."

"I guess that's what happens when your dreams get crushed too many times and the disappointment drags you under. You get strong because the alternative is to wither away and let everyone else step on you until you don't recognize yourself any longer." How had Camille gotten on a rant about independence and self-worth and the mess that was her life right now? She had to redirect the situation or they'd be talking about Carter and his pregnant girlfriend next...and that was *not* a subject she cared to discuss with Luke's wife. "So, enough about me and my misadventures in marriage. Tell me about your brother and sister, what you did in San Diego, and why you moved."

Twenty minutes later, Camille learned that Dominic and Estelle worked together in the family card stock business, and after Helena finished her Fine Arts degree and couldn't obtain a job in her field, she settled for retail work and waitressing.

"The jobs weren't anything to be thrilled about, but they paid the bills and I received discounts on my clothing and never went hungry." Helena laughed and picked up a ginger cookie. "Dominic and Estelle weren't happy about that."

"Oh?" Camille tried to catalogue what Helena had told her: parents were deceased, brother and sister worked in the family card stock business, and Helena had a degree in Fine Arts and no applicable job skills, so worked retail and waited tables. Hmm. "What was your maiden name?"

A pause, followed by a rush of air and a mumbled, "Montrey."

"Montrey. What a lovely name." *Dominic, Estelle, and Helena Montrey of San Diego. Good to know...* "And what exactly is a card

59

stock business? I imagine you sell paper and such, sort of like a stationery store?" She pictured all colors and sizes of paper, some for writing, others for drawing, and a heavier stock to create cards. There would be envelopes, too, all sizes and colors, and pens, pencils, markers. Camille thought she might enjoy perusing such a place... "What is it called? I might like to visit the next time I'm in San Diego." And she might like to meet Dominic and Estelle, get a first-hand look at the rest of the family.

A slight hesitation, a double clearing of her throat before Helena responded. "They sell cards and paper to wholesalers." Another pause. "So, there's no storefront."

"I see." It sounded very practical and not the creative venture she'd pictured. "And what did you do?"

"Packaged the cards mostly."

Camille leaned toward her, said in a curious voice, "Is that where you got the idea to write greeting cards?" She'd always been fascinated by those who could manufacture words or visuals from something that didn't yet exist. The woman blushed, looked away as if she'd rather not share the details of her writing aspirations. Poor thing, she'd probably failed many times. "Don't give up. If you work hard enough, are persistent, and never stop believing in your abilities, you'll find success. I know you will." Hadn't she told herself this for years? If only Camille had listened to her own words and believed them, she might not be a fifty-something woman with a limited skill set.

Helena met her gaze, blinked away tears. "Thank you."

"What sort of cards do you write? Are they humorous, romantic? Sad?" Emotion was the key to a good greeting card and Camille had spent enough time selecting the perfect sentiment via a card to know exactly what that meant. Her latest obsession happened to be cards from a writer-poet named Annabelle Grace. The woman's cards were separated under sections: Annabelle Grace Loves, Annabelle Grace Laughs, Annabelle Grace Cries, and Annabelle Grace Lives.

Helena shrugged. "All sorts. I'm still trying to get a feel for it."

"I understand." Emotions in card form were a delicate balance of poetry and self-expression. Carter was the king of finding the exact words to fit the occasion and he let the cards do his talking—and his double-talking. How many times had Camille been furious with him and then he'd presented her with a card that spoke of love, forgiveness, and an everlasting bond that would never be broken?

And then she'd go all soft and gooey like warm salted caramel drizzled on top of ice cream. It was those darn words that got her every time. An Annabelle Grace Loves card exclaimed, *You are the magic in my life. You are the strength behind me that makes all things possible. You are my life. My love. My forever.* Oh, yes, she'd received enough of these cards to memorize a few of her favorite phrases. Love, heart, and soul bound together.

And while the card was beautiful and touching, the intention was not. Carter had still been a cheater and a philanderer, and powerful words in a fancy card did not change that. Lately, she'd been the one selecting the cards and they hadn't been lovesick ones about heart and forever. No, they'd been determined, empowered, even angry in their refusal to be controlled or labeled by a person or a situation. They were from the Annabelle Grace Lives card line and spoke of betrayal and disappointment, but the message was one of strength and survival. Camille found the cards when she'd traveled to New York City and had been so moved by them she'd convinced Nicki to order several for the boutique. Last week, they'd learned the company that supplied the cards would soon include magnets, bookmarks, posters, and a book compiled of the writer-poet's work.

How exciting! Camille had considered contacting the woman but hesitated. She'd never reached out to a writer before. What would she say and how would she say it? A person like that probably had an auto-correct button in their brain. But the cards didn't sound like that at all. Every one of them was heartfelt and honest, not hoity-toity or superior acting. Maybe she'd write to this person and ask for advice on how to pursue a career in the greeting card field. Helena appeared too shy to reach out to a successful person like Annabelle Grace, and if Camille garnered a response, that might create a bond between her and Helena.

And that could prove very useful when she dug around in Helena's past. Camille sipped her coffee, smiled at Luke's wife. Yes, very useful indeed.

Chapter 7

"If I'd known you were going to walk into my life, I might have been a little more careful with my bank account."

A grin accompanied the comment, making it difficult to tell if Luke were teasing, serious, or both. That was the thing about him: Helena couldn't always tell. Yes, he'd admitted to opening up with her in ways he'd never imagined doing, and it wasn't hard to realize a man like Luke Donovan didn't talk about emotion and fear very often. He'd done it with her and, to some degree, she'd done the same with him. The big fear sitting in her belly right next to their baby was the fact that she'd been dishonest with him, and while her intent *had* been honorable—at least in her eyes—he wouldn't think so. There was still so much she didn't know or understand about him, so much she wanted to learn... But he wasn't an easy read and she wondered if that weren't intentional. "Is that your way of letting me know we're broke?"

He trailed a finger to her belly, traced little circles over her flesh. "Broke? Of course not." The laugh came next. "But who couldn't use more?"

Helena homed in on his face, said in a tight voice, "Maybe you should have married a woman with money." Luke might be teasing but she didn't see the humor in it, not when she *was* a woman with money who'd been targeted before because of it.

Another laugh followed by a kiss on her belly. "Yeah, maybe I should have. No need to worry about bills or college for the kid, just one big party. And a Harley." He slid her a look, his lips curving into a broad smile. "I've always wanted one of those, but they're damned expensive. I could have two: a touring bike and a cruiser. Hmm." Three more kisses followed by a gentle "There's only one problem. You're the one I want."

And I have enough money to buy you five motorcycles and so much more... When he learned of her wealth, would he still want *her* or would the wanting shift to what he could have because of her? Maybe he'd end up resenting her because she had money, call her a "have" and accuse her of not knowing what "being without" felt like. Oh, she knew exactly what that felt like because while she'd had clothes and a house and material wealth, she'd never had a sense of belonging or being accepted for herself. "Money wouldn't make you happy. It might give you a temporary high and take you around the world, but life's got to be about more than that, doesn't it?"

He sat up, the pale blueness of his eyes shifting to silver. "I've only heard two types of people say money won't make you happy." His gaze narrowed. "The ones who have too much money or the ones who are so deep in debt they'll never dig out. Helena, is there something you haven't told me?"

No, she could not tell him yet. It was still too soon. Just a little while longer... But the longer she waited, the worse it would be when she finally told him. Then what? Was it worth the risk? Still, hadn't he just pretty much admitted he wouldn't mind a woman with money? Lots of it? The pain of remembering her ex-fiancé's betrayal won out. "What do you mean?"

Luke eased back against the wooden headboard, rubbed his jaw. "I think the question is pretty straightforward. Is there something you haven't told me?"

She sat up, too, forced a smile. "Like?" Hadn't her sister and brother played these types of games with her when they wanted to avoid an answer? And hadn't she hated it? Yes, she had, but this was different...wasn't it?

He blew out a sigh that sounded an awful lot like disgust. "Look, I realize we got involved way too fast and skipped over a few areas we should have discussed." Another sigh, this one softer, his tone gentler. "I don't regret any of it, but we can't hide things because we're embarrassed about them or wish they hadn't happened."

"I know." She did know and once she was one hundred percent sure her money didn't matter, she'd tell him. And then she'd find a way to exchange vows again, *this time for real*. She couldn't tell him their marriage was a fake, that she'd paid a coworker to pretend he was a minister. Luke would not understand that she'd only been trying to protect him and give him a way out in case he grew tired of her and his married situation. Once she knew for certain he wasn't after her money *and* wanted this life, she'd convince him to renew their vows. Nobody would ever have to know...

"So—" he held out a hand, squeezed hers when she placed it in his. "Honesty, right? I'll go first. I've blown a lot of money over the years and got myself into a scrape or two that required a little...assistance. Rogan helped me out, tried to convince me to save or at least not spend more than I made. I didn't listen; why would I when it was always about the next good time?" A dull blush spread from his neck to his cheeks. "Tossing money around gets the girl's interest every time, but you were different. You didn't act like you cared about money and you didn't seem to want fancy dinners or gifts or—"

"Because I didn't." She leaned toward him, stroked his cheek. "And I don't." Helena held up her left hand. "This ring wasn't necessary." A row of diamonds glittered from the band. "I would have been happy with a simple band, minus the diamonds."

"You deserved more." His jaw twitched. "But there was no way you were getting less."

"Luke, all I want is you. Us. Our baby. Money can't buy those."

"I know, and I'm going to take my brother's advice and learn about saving and money management and all of those other terms I used to hate." He lifted her hand to his lips, kissed each finger. "I'm going to be practical, another word I've always hated, but I'm going to do it because it makes sense and it's the right thing to do."

"Thank you."

His lips pulled into a gentle smile. "It's your turn. I want you to tell me the truth." He paused, cleared his throat. "No matter how bad it is, I want you to tell me." One more throat clearing before he spoke the words that said he'd never guess the truth and might not believe it once she told him. "Are you in financial trouble? Like, deep debt? It's okay if you are, but you have to tell me so I can help. Okay?"

There would be countless times after when she'd wonder what life might have looked like if she'd confessed the whole tale, including the ex-fiancé who'd only wanted her money and the siblings who were more interested in production times than family bonding. Could he have understood or at least forgiven her when the anger subsided? She'd never know because she changed the truth and offered up a different version—one that did not implicate her as anything other than a victim.

"Yes, I did make some bad financial choices. I trusted the wrong person." *An ex-fiancé who wanted her money more than he wanted her.* "The experience made it hard to trust and it's still hard." She willed him to understand what she couldn't say.

"I'm sorry you had to go through that. How bad was it?" His voice dipped, spilled sympathy. "Bankruptcy?"

Helena shook her head, settled her gaze on the opening of his shirt. "Not quite that bad, but bad enough." Bad enough to cost her half a house, a car, chunks of money, her self-esteem, and the ability to trust. It was the last two that were unforgivable.

"Is that why you left San Diego? Too many bad memories?"

Another nod. At least this was true. "I wanted to start fresh where no one knew me or judged me." Her gaze inched to his, held it. "People are judged all the time, by what they wear, how they look, what kind of car they drive... Society deems them worthy or unworthy based on profession, education...who knows what? A friend once told me that net worth does not equal self-worth and it took a long time to understand that, but I finally got it."

"When I look at you, I see a million dollars in your smile, ten million in your touch, one hundred million in your heart." Luke placed a hand over her heart, smiled. "I love you, Helena Donovan. No matter what, never forget that."

When the tears came she couldn't stop them from running down her cheeks, spilling onto her shirt. "I'm sorry," she said, shoulders shaking, words snuffed out by the tears. "So sorry."

"It's okay. We're in this together and I'll help you any way I can. If you want, I'll even ask Rogan to get involved. He's a pain but he means well, and the guy knows his numbers. If you're in a jam, I know he can help. You're family now, and family helps one another."

LUKE DROVE to Rogan's that night because he needed his brother's help. Rogan was a hard ass who would no doubt point out the mistakes and miscalculations in his brother's past, but in the end, he'd offer advice and a plan that made sense. It was the lectures Luke dreaded. Couldn't the guy get to the point and forget the commentary? Just this once? Of course not—his brother wasn't made that way, so Luke sat through the scowl and the lesson about not blowing six hundred dollars on a leather jacket when you only had one hundred until payday, even if the leather was Italian. Big sigh and more talk about not spending money you didn't have and staying away from credit cards. Okay, he got it.

"I agree with everything you've said and if you give me a budget, I'll follow it." Luke studied the label on his beer bottle. "I've got two other people to consider now, and I don't want to screw up."

"Good." Rogan eyed him. "Glad to hear it."

Why did his brother sound like he didn't believe him? "I'll do it, you'll see." And then, because he couldn't stand to hear one more word about savings and debt, and because he'd carried regret around too long, he said, "I'm sorry I bailed on you when Dad and Mom got into trouble. There's no excuse and it was a crappy thing to do." He sipped his beer, leaned back against the kitchen counter. "I've never worried about doing the right thing or how my actions might affect someone else. Hell, I never even considered the consequences for half the stuff I did." He shot a glance at Rogan, shrugged. "I could go on, but you probably know my failings better than I do."

Rogan's lips pulled into a faint grin. "Probably so."

Another shrug. "Figured as much. Did you ever think there's a reason for so many screw-ups?" Luke had realized the truth years ago and once he admitted it, he'd gone full throttle on the self-gratification and risk-taking and to hell with everyone else—especially his brother.

"A reason, huh?" Rogan rubbed his jaw. "You mean other than stupidity and immaturity?"

Luke shook his head. "Funny. I won't deny either, but they're not it." Pause. "You are."

"Me? What's that supposed to mean?" Rogan's blue gaze narrowed on him, the brackets around his mouth deepening.

"You're the son every parent wishes he had. I, on the other hand, am the one every parent wishes he could ignore." There, he'd finally said it. For years, he'd felt inferior when compared to his oldest brother. Even Charlotte came in far behind Rogan. "You always did everything right. Didn't run away from a tough choice, helped Mom and Dad, loaned me money, and I'm guessing you helped Charlotte, too. There just weren't any missteps and for a guy like me, that can get really tiring."

He dragged a hand through his hair, pushed out more truths. "I spent a lot of years running from my dissatisfaction with myself and my choices. But a year or so ago I got tired of it all. The running, the women, the life that was about finding satisfaction and never achieving it. I had to finally admit *I* was the problem, my lifestyle was a problem, but that didn't mean I knew what to do about it." His voice softened, and he thought of the woman who'd changed his life. "Then

I met Helena. I know she's too good for me, know I don't deserve her, but I'm not going to give her up. I can't give her up."

Rogan finished his beer, pulled out two more from the fridge, and handed one to Luke. "First, I'm not that perfect. Trust me on that one, and if you don't believe me, ask my wife. I just hide my issues better than you do. Second, about your wife...you sure fell hard and fast. What was it about her that sent you into a nosedive?"

The tone in his brother's voice said he was more than curious... He was suspicious. Of Luke or of Helena? "How about you stop dancing around the niceties and ask me straight out what you really want to know?"

Rogan twisted the cap off his beer, took a swig and studied Luke like he was about to begin another lecture. "I'm a numbers guy so I look at trends, facts, and statistics. Simple numbers, simple columns that add up and make sense. Nothing about you and Helena makes sense other than you landed in bed together and she ended up pregnant. But the rest? *Marrying* her? Planning this we'll-be-together-forever-life? You could never settle on a woman past a week and now you're ready to make a lifelong commitment?"

"Yeah, I am." Luke eyed his brother, clenched a fist against his thigh. "And how is this any different from you and Elizabeth? From what I hear, she was pregnant when you got married *and* there was a lapse in between when you weren't even together." Charlotte had filled him in on the couple's rough start and their mother gave him her version as well, beginning and ending with how much Rogan and Elizabeth were meant to be together—even if they didn't know it at first.

"Leave Elizabeth out of this." The tone in Rogan's voice said he was not going to tolerate anyone talking about his wife, not even his brother.

"Just answer me. I'm not judging, only asking."

"We're not talking about me right now. Everybody's wondering why you jumped into marriage and the consensus is she pushed you."

"The consensus? Are you all sitting around the table taking votes on how we ended up together?" The dull red inching up his brother's neck said that was pretty much exactly what they were doing. Damn them. He did not appreciate his family thinking the woman he loved was less than honorable. "She did not push me. *I'm* the one who pushed for the marriage."

His brother's lips stretched into what might be considered a smile if not for the coldness buried behind them. "Don't you know by now that the most effective measure a woman has of pushing is by looking like she's *not* pushing? You know, the ones who say they don't want a relationship and then end up pregnant? Happens every day. I've seen it too many times and I know you have, too. You can't blame any of us for wondering what this is really all about. This isn't fifty years ago where you had to marry the girl if you got her pregnant."

Luke pushed away from the counter, advanced toward Rogan and stopped when he was a punch away. "Helena is my wife and I love her and we're going to have a baby. We're going to make a life together and be happy. End of story." He crossed his arms over his chest, dared his brother to dispute those words.

"Good. Glad to hear about your wedded bliss and your future and all the happiness that goes with it. Nobody wants you to be unhappy, Luke. We just don't want you to get played either."

"Got it. And I appreciate the concern but it's not necessary. Helena and I are solid. She's the most honest person I've ever met." He could have no way of knowing how much he'd regret those words or wish he'd heeded Rogan's advice. For now, all he knew was that he and Helena were meant to be together and they were starting a family and a future together. And nothing else mattered.

Chapter 8

C arter always had an agenda, but the question was whether it was his own or his brother's. For much of her married life, Camille never knew because one was meshed with the other. Sometimes Carter's grand schemes required the assistance of his brother to extricate himself from the problems he created. Other times, Harrison, who had never been one for gentle persuasion, didn't hesitate to tell his brother exactly what was expected of him. Maybe that's why years and mistakes later, Carter still hadn't learned the consequences of his actions. Maybe he still thought a slow smile, an expensive gift, and a seductive glance would do the trick, and earn him forgiveness for all manner of misdeeds.

And that's exactly what he thought now as he stood before her in Nicki's boutique. The man hadn't dared attempt to visit their home, so he'd tried this tactic, believing she wouldn't make a scene. He might be right, or he might be wrong; that all depended on the lies that fell out of his mouth.

"This is a nice place, I like what she's done with it."

Camille followed his gaze as he took in the boutique: the salmon walls, the square-patterned carpeting, the wrought-iron chairs with plush seats arranged in a semicircle, the full-length oval mirrors on pedestals. The mood and décor spoke of a chic elegance, timeless and a tad trendy. "She's got an eye for good taste."

"Obviously." His gaze slid from her face to the tips of her designer heels, back to her face. "So do you."

Oh, for heaven's sake, was the man really going to attempt those overdone compliments? They might have worked when she'd been willing to accept the scraps he offered and ignored the gaps in their marriage. But not now, not any more. She wasn't interested in his words, his smile, or anything other than his signature on the divorce papers. Despite her lawyer's attempts to achieve the latter, he'd been unsuccessful. There'd been meetings, negotiations, back-and-forth disputes regarding property and settlement figures, but nothing to indicate they were anywhere near being done with this distasteful venture. How long should it take to reach an agreement? Camille ignored his comment, raised a brow, and homed in on Carter's designer watch. "Nicki has a husband who supports and encourages her, despite two babies at home. *That's* true partnership, Carter, and we never had that." Camille highlighted a line on the inventory sheet and flipped the page. What on earth did this man want and how could she get him to leave? Nicki was due in soon and Camille wanted the man long gone before her friend arrived.

Carter placed his hands on the counter, manicured nails gleaming under the low light of the boutique. "I know I was wrong." His words dripped misery and regret. "Everything's always been too damn easy for me. I never learned what it meant to not get anything I wanted. If I thought it, I had it." His blue gaze simmered with intensity. "Until now."

She ignored the heat in his words and the fact that they were directed at her. How many times had he played this game before and how many times had she believed him? "I really don't understand what this has to do with me." And then because she could not keep her mouth shut, she added, "Did your little sex toy realize you aren't perfect? Did she not praise you enough?"

A burst of red swept from his neck to his cheeks. "Cammie...

You're right. I was a fool and Mindy's just a girl, not a woman... You always made me better than I was. I need that... I *want* that..."

"Really?" Well, this was an interesting turnabout, and one she hadn't expected and didn't quite believe. "Unless I'm mistaken, you're going to be a father."

More red colored his cheeks. "I am, but who knows if the child's even mine? It could belong to someone else; you never know about a person like that..."

Camille might detest Mindy, but for Carter to spew words he absolutely knew were false to save himself was disgusting. He had an angle and it wasn't about Mindy. It was all about him. "Stop lying, Carter. You're not interested in anything but yourself, and anyone *but* yourself. So, just tell me what happened, and we'll go from there. Did big brother have a talk with you? Did he tell you to break it off with Mindy and get things right with me or he'd cut you off? I don't imagine a life of reduced circumstances would look appealing to anyone, especially a pregnant girlfriend who thinks you're a king." She spotted the truth of her words the second his shoulders slumped, his eyes grew dim, and his lips pulled down. He was such a handsome man, but so damn weak...

"I'll admit, Harrison might have commented about my relationship with Mindy and how he's not happy about the divorce, but he's opened my eyes. He's made me see that we belong together, that we'll always belong together, no matter the difficulties we've had."

If she could lift the cash register, she'd hurl it at him. *"Difficulties?* Difficulties that were brought on by you and your inability to control your desire to sleep with anyone and then to lie about it. I don't like that girl, but she adores you, believes you care about her, too. And maybe you do. Maybe you need someone like that who'll fawn over you, tell you that you're the light of her existence. I don't know, and I don't care, because it doesn't matter. What does matter is that you and I—us—we're done. You are *not* my light. In fact, I'd rather spend the afternoon with your brother talking about his damnable roses and stock prices, and you know how I feel about him."

"Cammie, please—"

She cut him off. "The difference between you and Harrison is that he's never tried to pretend he was anything other than a horrible, controlling man, while you put on a smile and let everyone believe you care, including your children. Grow up, Carter. Be a man. Do the right thing by this baby for once in your miserable life. Give me the divorce and take care of Mindy and the baby. You made the mess; now you fix it. Who knows? Maybe the three of you will grow up together." She offered a cold smile as she pointed toward the door. "Miracles do happen."

WHEN ROGAN ASKED Luke if he were interested in hiring on to remodel the old house he and Elizabeth bought, he'd thought his brother was testing him—or joking. The question was either a way to find out if Luke had matured and grown dependable in the last several years, or it was an attempt to stuff humor into their relationship.

Both possibilities annoyed the crap out of Luke and he let his brother know it five seconds after Rogan asked the question. What he hadn't anticipated was that his brother really did mean exactly what he'd said.

"You're saying you want me to remodel your house?" Luke stood in Rogan's kitchen two days after their money management conversation, arms crossed over his chest, frown on his face. "Me? The brother you once called reckless, undependable, and irresponsible?"

Rogan shrugged, the brackets around his mouth deepening. "Yup."

Luke scratched his head, squinted. "What am I missing? Is this a trick question?" He sighed, dragged a hand through his hair. "You don't trust me to do the right thing, Rogan. You've never trusted me, so why would you hand over a job that involves the largest asset you own?"

There was such a long pause, Luke almost asked the question again. When he opened his mouth to repeat it, his brother cut him off. "Because I've been thinking about our talk the other day and I think you've changed. And you've been fixing stuff around the house for Mom that she didn't even know needed fixing. Plus, a wife and a baby on the way make us see life from a different angle, and maybe we've both changed."

"Huh." Luke narrowed his gaze on his brother. "Why do I feel there's another piece to this complicated puzzle?"

Rogan looked away, settled his gaze on the kitchen table. "Elizabeth isn't used to living in a rundown house with lights that don't work, holes in the walls, and daylight coming through the upstairs ceiling. I've got three water leaks in the ceiling and the damn bathroom door doesn't even close. She never complains but she deserves better than this, and even if I had the time—" he slid a gaze to Luke "—I don't have the skill sets you do. I'm good with painting a wall and ripping up carpeting, but installing a dishwasher? Replacing tile and patching a roof? I'm better at patching balance sheets and fixing people's finances."

Luke let out a laugh. "So, you're admitting there's something I'm better at than you?" Now this was a first. The old Rogan would never have confessed to any faults, or to his brother's abilities.

"If I do, will you agree to take on the job?" Pause. "And start working on it ASAP? It won't be long before we have a new addition and I'm not talking about a new room."

"This place needs a lot of work. It's going to take money and a crew." Luke scratched his jaw, studied the ceiling with its water spots and chipped plaster. "A lot of both."

A burst of red covered his brother's cheeks. "Yeah, about that..."

"Let me guess. You want to pay me in food and do most of the work myself?" If he didn't have a pregnant wife to think about, he probably would have considered it.

"Money's not an issue." More red, inching to his ears. "That's not true. Money *is* an issue, but it's my issue..."

Luke scratched his head, stared at his brother. When had he ever known Rogan to act unsure about *anything*? He was a take-charge kind of guy who didn't flip-flop or hesitate and acted like he had the answer even when he had no clue. So, what was going on? "You know you're not making any sense, right?"

His brother let out a sigh that stopped just short of annoyed. "I don't like to talk about it so I'm only going to say it once." One more big sigh, this one definitely annoyed. "Elizabeth has money. A lot of it."

"Oh." It wasn't that the Donovans had anything against wealth or the people who had it, but when you grew up with second-hand everything because you couldn't afford brand-new, well, it left a mark on you. And while you didn't want to admit it, it made you resentful of the people who didn't know about hand-me-downs or doing without. Yeah, Luke was glad Helena didn't have money. Not that he liked her near-bankruptcy status, but at least he could relate to that. But a woman with a big bank account? Maybe a trust fund? No thanks. Not in this universe.

"I didn't find out until it was too late and then..."

"Too late as in she was already pregnant, or you were already in love with her?" Luke wanted to see his brother try to get out of this one, so he added an extra zing. "Or both?"

"Go to hell."

Luke laughed. "That's what I figured. Too far gone on both accounts. So, Elizabeth has money. It could be worse." When Rogan glared at him, Luke shrugged and muttered, "Or not." Maybe their attitude toward money would have been different if they hadn't grown up in the same town as the almighty Alexanders and the reminder of just how much the Donovans didn't have. Or maybe their father had been just a bit too proud and disdainful of those who didn't have to struggle as much as they did.

Rogan shrugged. "It's part of the package and I have to get used to it."

He hadn't said "had" as in past tense, which meant he was still adjusting. "I see. And just to show her you didn't care about or want her money, you bought this place?" Luke swept a hand around the room. "Is it a test? See if she'll stay once she realizes you're never going to have money like the Alexanders?" The look on Rogan's face said there might be a speck of truth in those words but when he spoke, it wasn't that at all.

"I didn't want her money and we agreed we'd live on what we made with our jobs, not her inheritance. But I don't want her living like this: drywall falling from the ceiling, worn-out plumbing, missing floorboards. I finally had to admit it was more about pride and that wasn't fair to her or the baby. Just wait, you'll see what compromise and owning up to your own shortcomings are all about." He paused, said in a quiet voice, "Especially when a child's involved. You want to do right by your family and that's when you have to look at your actions and question why you're really doing them."

Wow, his brother was admitting he didn't know everything. Imagine that? "I've already had to do that a few times. Not my strong suit, but I did it." Like opening up and sharing, even the parts he didn't want to share.

"Okay, then you get it." Rogan pushed away from the counter, made his way across the room, and eased a long paper tube from the top of the fridge. "Here are the plans for the house. I'd like you to take a look, see what you can do, and hire out the rest." He removed the plans from the tube, spread them on the kitchen table. "Elizabeth and I want to make you the foreman on this job." Rogan glanced at Luke. "I've got a list of subcontractors. Tate's vetted them and—"

"Damn! Am I really going to have to work with that guy?" Tate Alexander, Savior to the Simple Man?

Rogan shrugged. "It's not like he'll be handing you a screwdriver because he wouldn't know the difference between a flathead and a Phillips, but he's a good resource for the subcontractors."

"Crap. Not what I wanted to hear." Luke cursed under his breath, mumbled, "Pain-in-the-ass pretty boy." He'd like to list all of Tate

Alexander's faults, but the damn guy didn't have any, other than he was too rich and too self-assured.

Rogan laughed. "Give the guy time. He kind of grows on you."

"Sure." Luke scowled. "Like moss or mold."

Another laugh. "Yeah, but he's good for Charlotte."

The guy *was* good for their sister: kept her calm, smiling, even-tempered. "I guess. Charlotte drove me to the property they bought and showed me the plans. Wow! Talk about a killer house." He whistled. "She said Alexander had grander ideas for the place, but she had him tone it down. Three fireplaces? Really?"

"For a guy who grew up in a mansion, it probably does seem small. Point is, he's shaving bedrooms, floor space, and whatever else Charlotte wants." Rogan rubbed his jaw, nodded. "The guy loves her, and I guess we're going to have to start using his first name instead of Pain in the Ass, Jerk, Pretty Boy..." He cleared his throat, said in a quiet voice, "Speaking of Pretty Boy..." When Luke raised a brow, Rogan grinned. "Seriously, the guy has contacts and if that means we get the job done better and faster, then we're using them."

"What would Dad say?" What *would* he say?

"I hope he'd realize Tate's one of the good guys even if he is an Alexander."

Chapter 9

Sometimes a person has to hide their silly ideas from friends and family, lest those individuals feel compelled to judge and laugh. At least, that's what Camille thought as she parked the car and stepped through the door of Victor's Ballroom Dancing, located 22 miles from Reunion Gap in a town called Granite. She'd registered for the class last week after reading an article about a fifty-something-year-old woman who'd drawn up a list of ten accomplishments she wanted to achieve before her time on this earth ended. The only requirement was that each item on the list must help her grow on an emotional or spiritual level.

Ballroom dancing was top on Camille's list though she'd never admit it to Rose or her brother Oliver. She'd wanted to take classes years ago, but Carter thought them too time-consuming and unnecessary. Maybe they were for a man who had no interest in learning new things unless they involved young women and sex. She squashed that thought a second after it landed in her brain. A growth-inspiring accomplishment should not be mired in anger and harsh thoughts.

Camille worked her way to a table where a slender brunette with hair piled on top of her head and heavy black eyeliner signed in new members. Her name was Regina and she spoke with a French accent, though she'd slipped on a few of the vowels, making Camille wonder if the accent were feigned. The instructor was a middle-aged man named Victor Evergreen. He reminded her of a dancer or a magician with his slight build, slicked-back hair, pencil-thin mustache, and dramatic hand gestures. The smile and the perfect diction said he was indeed playing a part, one he enjoyed very much.

"Camille, welcome." Victor clasped her hand and bowed. "A true delight and my deepest gratitude for joining us." His dark eyes sparkled. "We shall have a grand time, of that you may be certain." He released her hand, said in a voice smothered with enthusiasm, "Please feel free to mingle and we'll begin shortly."

"Thank you." The man's warm greeting relaxed her, made her anticipate the class. Maybe she would enjoy herself and next time the Donovan clan pushed aside the furniture to dance, she'd join them instead of making excuses about a swollen ankle or lower back pain. She glanced at the packet the young woman with the dubious French accent had given her and was reading about proper shoes and ballroom attire when a familiar voice called her name.

"Camille?"

She turned and came eye to eye with Frederick Strong, legal counsel for HA Properties, Inc. "Frederick?" Heat seeped to her cheeks, spread to her forehead. "What...what are you doing here?" Talk about an uncomfortable situation. She'd traveled two towns away, so no one would recognize her and now Harrison Alexander's lawyer was here. Oh, but this was humiliating.

The blush that matched his pink shirt said he wasn't thrilled to be seen either. "My niece is getting married in a few months, and I promised her a dance." He cleared his throat, adjusted his bowtie. "I can't disappoint her, and I don't want to embarrass her, so—" his thin lips pulled into a faint smile "—here I am."

Frederick Strong had worked for Harrison at HA Properties, Inc., for years, and yet she knew little about him. Oh, she'd seen him at the office and they'd shared a few conversations about travel and the types of tomatoes that made the best marinara sauce—the travel was firsthand knowledge while the tomato preference was gleaned from a magazine article he'd read. Still, other than those few conversations and one or two run-ins at The Oak Table or the grocery store, she wouldn't say she *knew* the man. There was no wife or children, not that she'd heard about anyway.

Would Frederick stay with Tate, or would he migrate to whatever camp of deception and greed Harrison had set up? There was only one way to find out and while the man *could* lie to her, she didn't think he would. She offered him a small smile, tapped the dance booklet against her hand. "My nephew is big on loyalty and doing right by people." A raised brow, followed by a calculating "I wouldn't want to see him blindsided because of his trusting nature. Tell me, when Harrison attempts to recruit you, if he hasn't already done so, will you go with him, or will you stay with my nephew?"

Frederick Strong squared his shoulders, making him appear three inches taller, and spoke in a voice that left no doubt he was not used to having his intentions *or* his integrity questioned. "I'm staying with Tate. Harrison and I worked together for years, and while I didn't always agree with his methods, I was never personally involved or witnessed any wrongdoing."

Camille raised a brow. The man wanted to feign integrity? Hah! "How convenient for you. I can't imagine how you managed such a feat unless you closed your eyes." She stepped closer, lowered her voice. "Harrison Alexander is a horrible, devious manipulator who doesn't care who he hurts, including his own family. If you think you're absolved from the stain of his sin because you didn't *personally* witness it, you're wrong. You had to know the man was up to no good, and I'll bet you did nothing to try and stop him."

The man narrowed his blue gaze on her, his thin lips a straight line. "I suspected he had side deals, but I was never involved with them, nor was I able to find any documentation of wrongdoing—" he paused, cleared his throat "—until Tate took over. Once he started looking, we found the inconsistencies...and acted on them."

"Oh?" She waited for him to offer more, but those thin lips remained clamped shut. "Fine. If you don't want to tell me, I'll ask my nephew. Tate and I have a very good relationship." Camille sniffed. "How sad you didn't exercise a bit more of that integrity you're so keen to show off when Harrison was conducting all manner of misdeeds. Looking the other way and not asking questions does not absolve you, no matter what your conscience tells you." And with that, she turned and headed to the other end of the room, checked her watch, and waited for the ballroom dance class to begin.

While Camille was able to ignore Frederick Strong during the class, the man's words remained with her through the night and into the next day. *I suspected he had side deals, but I was never involved with them, nor was I able to find any documentation of wrongdoing...we found the inconsistencies...and acted on them.* Why hadn't the man simply shared an inconsistency or two? What would have been the harm? It's not like she'd blabber his findings all over town. She knew about keeping confidences and secrets, had done so for years. All she'd been trying to determine was the level of loyalty Frederick Strong had toward her nephew. Was he backing him because the board wanted Tate at the helm of HA Properties, Inc., or did the lawyer believe in her nephew's vision, character, and integrity? Who knew? Apparently, the man wasn't going to share details that might help Camille determine his intentions. Well, she planned to put her investigative talents to work and find out.

Ferreting out truths had become her mission, and Frederick Strong's role at HA Properties, Inc., was a truth she planned to uncover. But there was a more pressing *investigation* she'd undertaken: finding out Helena Montrey's backstory, including family, life, and anything else that occurred before she met Luke. She'd contacted Lester Conroy last week and put him in charge of reconstructing the woman's past. If his findings matched what she'd told them, then Camille would relax and welcome her new "niece" into the Donovan clan. However, if there were discrepancies—especially, significant ones—then that would be a whole other issue, and a huge problem, considering there was a baby involved. She recalled her conversation with the private investigator who'd been happy to hear from her but cautious about her request.

Camille, gathering information on someone can be dangerous. It can ruin lives.

Oh, Lester, why the melodrama? You've been doing it for years.

There'd been a long pause and then, *And I've caused my own share of heartache and sorrow. I got bushels full of regret, too. I should have known when to refuse a client and I let it go too far.* Another pause followed by a painful, *Everybody paid the price.*

I need your help. My nephew's future depends upon it. He brought home a pregnant wife we know nothing about, and her story about who she is and where she's been is flimsy.

Can you be more specific?

The woman's got class and breeding, and that means she's got a past my nephew doesn't know about. We have to find out what she's hiding before it's too late.

Isn't the woman pregnant? Sounds like it might already be too late.

It's never too late to extricate oneself from a bad relationship, unless he's fallen so deeply in love with her that it would be more painful to sever the relationship than to continue it.

The drawl in his Texas accent turned softer. *Are you talking about your nephew, Camille? Or would those words pertain to yourself?*

I guess both. Will you help him, Lester? Please? I planned to attempt the investigation myself, but that could be a disaster.

You could do some basic groundwork for me, gather details, make observations. But the question is, can you be objective and take the emotion from the situation? A good investigator observes; he does not interject emotion or the outcome he prefers. If you can do that, then I'll accept your help. If you can't, then it's best for both of us if you let me handle it.

I'll do it.

~

THE DONOVANS WERE a family and if Helena was very lucky, she would become a part of that family. As the days rolled by and winter settled into spring, Helena eased into life in Reunion Gap. Most mornings, she had breakfast with Rose, and then Elizabeth would head over with her sketchpads and drawing utensils. They sat in the sunroom, each lost in her own world as Elizabeth drew and Helena wrote. For Elizabeth it was about finding the perfect subject for her next creation, whether it be a flower, a leaf, or the intricate details of a vine, and then bringing it to life.

Helena's world involved words: heartfelt, sincere, honest. She'd given up trying to produce work for the Annabelle Grace Lives and Annabelle Grace Cries lines because it was difficult to pretend anger, resentment, and sorrow when she felt none of those. She was happy, at peace—in love. That's why she'd begun producing for the Annabelle Grace Loves line again, and while Dominic and Estelle weren't pleased about it, they did agree that at least she was contributing work on a steady basis. What would they say if they knew she were going to have a baby with a man she met fewer than six months ago? A man who thought they were married and knew nothing about her real life?

Soon, Helena would have to tell Luke who she really was and that the Annabelle Grace Loves card he bought her the other day was one she'd written. What would he say to that? She believed Luke loved her and she even believed he wanted to be a father. But what if he tired of the domestic life? It wouldn't be about him or even about them anymore, not once the baby came. Elizabeth said she'd read it was important for couples to remain couples and not lose themselves in the baby. But how did successful parents manage that? Camille Alexander told Helena that Jameson and Nicki Price were perfect examples of two people who still enjoyed date nights and spending time together—without children. She'd said more people should be like that, should not forget what brought them together in the first place.

Camille had a lot to say about a lot of things, and Helena was tempted to ask her how she could be so knowledgeable and yet had acted on none of that knowledge in her own relationship? Of course, she'd never ask but she wanted to... The woman intimidated and unsettled her. Was that intentional or simply Camille Alexander's personality? Either way, when Luke's aunt paid them a visit, usually unannounced, Helena ended up with heartburn or a headache, sometimes both.

She glanced at Elizabeth, whose blonde head was bent over her sketchpad, fingers busy creating a crocus. Elegant, poised, and beautiful, Rogan's wife possessed a gentleness that drew Helena to her, made her wish the other family members were a bit more reserved and less opinionated. Elizabeth and Rogan were a good couple and it was obvious they loved each other very much. Did the Donovans think she and Luke were a good couple, and was it obvious they loved each other very much? Or did they wonder if they were together because of the baby or worse, because of Luke's reckless lifestyle? It was hard to tell and while there were moments when Helena *wanted* to know, there were more moments when she did not.

Elizabeth glanced up from her sketchpad. "Know what I was just thinking?"

Helena shook her head. "No idea."

A smile inched across Elizabeth's lips. "This time next year, I'll be drawing our babies and you'll be writing about them." She placed a hand on her large, round belly. "I'm so glad you're here. It's exciting to know our children will grow up together." Her brows pinched, her voice turned melancholy. "I always wished for a brother or sister, even a cousin, so I didn't have to be alone."

"My siblings are older than I am, so in a lot of ways I was an only child." Helena placed both hands on her belly, massaged it. "And when my parents died a few years apart, I always hoped my brother and sister would take over, kind of become the parents." She let the sadness spill out. "That never happened."

"Well, we're going to make sure our children don't grow up alone." Elizabeth leaned forward, laid a hand on Helena's arm. "Rogan and I don't want this baby to be an only child, but if that's how it turns out, at least there'll be a cousin close by."

"Yes, at least there's that." Oh, how she wished she weren't keeping two gigantic secrets from Luke, ones that could affect her destiny and the baby's. What if he couldn't accept the fact that she'd lied about her real identity? What if he viewed it as a betrayal? Would his feelings for her wither and die? She swallowed, sucked in air. He'd held her last night, spoken of his love for her and the baby with such emotion, she'd cried. She could not lose that love and yet, she could not continue sharing a life with him where he didn't know the truth.

"Helena? Are you okay?" Elizabeth's gaze shot to her belly. "Is it the baby?"

The poor baby had become the excuse for every uncomfortable situation or unwanted response. It wasn't right or fair to the child, and yet Helena had let the Donovans' assumptions stand uncorrected. The quiet spells, the indigestion and headaches were not about the baby at all. No, they were about the secrets that remained hidden that could tear her and Luke apart, kill their love, and the future of their family. That's what made her sick and a bit too quiet, that's what worried her deep into the night, long after Luke had fallen into a post lovemaking sleep.

"Helena? Should I call Luke?"

"No. I'm fine." Helena dragged her gaze to Elizabeth, spotted the concern and anxiety on her face. "I guess sometimes I think about how much I want to be a part of this family, and I don't know if they'll ever really accept me." There was truth in her words, even if they weren't the reason for her upset. "They're a tight family and they're loyal. You can tell they stand behind one another even if they don't agree." Pause, a deep breath before she rushed on. "And heaven help anyone who hurts one of them."

"Yes, heaven help that person." Elizabeth leaned back in her chair, let out a soft sigh. "I've been on the end of that anger and I never want to be there again." Her voice drifted, turned sad and wistful. "I thought I'd lost Rogan forever. Who would have thought Tate Alexander would come to the rescue, huh? That man is worth a whole bank vault of gold, no matter what the men have to say about him." Elizabeth *tsk-tsked.* "I think they're jealous of his kindness. And his manners...his looks..."

Tate Alexander *was* handsome, charming, attentive, and gracious, with a gentleness about him that made him approachable. He'd made several efforts to talk with her but if Luke were in the vicinity, the efforts sizzled. "Charlotte's a lucky woman."

Elizabeth shook her head, let out a soft laugh. "Oh, she is, and she knows it. I guess he'd planned to take her to Hawaii for an official honeymoon, but then you and Luke came home, and they postponed it." A pause, followed by "Charlotte was the one who wanted to wait, said she couldn't leave, not with a long-lost brother coming home with a new wife and a baby on the way."

Helena frowned. "Does Luke know? I'm sure he'd never want her to miss a trip to Hawaii because of him." Was seeing her brother again the real reason Charlotte cancelled? Or did it have more to do with not trusting Helena or her motives? She'd seen the way Luke's sister watched her, like the woman was waiting for her to make a misstep. But why? Luke had confessed that his family was an inquisitive bunch, but he'd also said they possessed suspicious natures that had grown worse after the disaster with their father. Apparently, Jonathan Donovan had not been inquisitive or suspicious enough, and that had been his downfall.

"Luke knows. So does Rogan." Elizabeth rolled her eyes. "You can imagine the comments those two made. I think Luke said something about how it was pretty bad when your wife refused your honeymoon trip to Hawaii, and Rogan said the new house he's building probably drained his funds." A big sigh and a shrug. "I did not hesitate to tell my husband he was being petty and childish, and I didn't appreciate his prejudice toward people of means."

"Money doesn't guarantee a charmed life." Helena said. "People still die, heartbreak still happens, as does disappointment, loads of disappointment." Especially when you were being used to get to your money.

"You understand," Elizabeth said, her voice a mix of gentleness and resignation. "Most don't. Oh, they say they do, but once they hear you come from money or have come into it, they think your life is grand. One big party filled with every imaginable pleasure and no want." Her voice drifted. "But often, it's the exact opposite. You see, I know all about being raised in luxury, and what I remember most is the loneliness." She closed her eyes and massaged her belly. "Always on the outside looking in at life, yet never quite being able to touch it. Until I met Rogan. He's the most honorable man I've ever known and while our worlds were so different, love bridged that gap."

Elizabeth opened her eyes, met Helena's gaze. "And patience. It's the same for Tate and Charlotte, and I can see it will be the same for you and Luke. Your issue might not be money creating the divide, but different personalities and lifestyles." Her lips pulled into a faint smile. "I've heard stories about your husband and yet when he's with you, all I see is a man consumed with love and the need to protect."

There'd been enough reference to "stories" about Luke that she knew they were true, knew also that she didn't want to hear about them. And she hadn't missed the looks from the women in town that said they'd either been involved with him or *wanted* to be involved with him. Luke ignored all of it, but Helena couldn't pretend her husband's past exploits, combined with his rugged appeal, didn't make him a target for those who didn't care about a pregnant wife. She pushed aside thoughts of other women, blew out a long breath. "I feel the same about him."

"Good." Elizabeth glanced at Helena's notebook. "Don't ever give up your passion, no matter what."

"I won't." Writing and creating lived in her soul and she could not give up either.

"I think you're going to do very well with your cards." Elizabeth offered a smile. "I've only read a few, but they move me. There's real emotion there, not just cute words that rhyme." She paused, her gaze narrowing on the notebook. "They kind of remind me of Annabelle Grace cards. I love those cards."

Thank you. "Yes," Helena said. "Me, too."

Chapter 10

"What do you think about Anastasia? Or Evangeline? Or maybe we should call her Veronica."

Luke lay beside Helena on the bed, his head resting against her belly. They'd gone to the doctor today, heard the baby's heartbeat... *Their baby.* She stroked Luke's hair, buried her fingers in its softness. Would their baby have light brown hair with golden highlights? Pale blue eyes? Would their baby be a girl or a boy? "What if our baby's a boy? I kind of like Lucas John." Helena traced the line of his jaw, trailed a finger to his lips.

His strong arm circled her expanding waist, pulled her closer. "Lucas, huh? I never gave it much thought but then I wasn't in the habit of discussing baby names."

"Lucas is a strong name and I've always liked it." Her voice shifted, filled with emotion. "But now I've become a bit obsessed with it."

His laughter spilled through the room, rich, deep. "Lucas could work as long as he's not a pain in the butt like his father. He's got to be disciplined, practical, and book-smart. More like his Uncle Rogan."

Was he serious? Did Luke find himself lacking when compared to his brother? "I hope he's exactly like his father," she whispered. "Kind, compassionate, and gentle. Very loyal."

"That's the Luke you see now, not the one who felt he had to prove himself by being headstrong, reckless, and pretty much an inconsiderate jerk."

She let out a slow breath. "I'd call that growing pains, and it was all worth it."

He traced tiny circles on the side of her belly, kissed the center of a circle. "I'm hoping we can move out and get our own place once the baby comes. That still gives us time to save and look around." Pause, followed by a hesitant "Tate said he knows a couple places for rent and I guess he has real estate that he'd be willing to sell." Long-suffering sigh. "Damn, but I hate to be beholden to him."

Why couldn't people see that sometimes others offered because they really wanted to do it, no strings attached? "He's family now. Did you ever think this is his way of being part of the family? Of trying to show you he wants to be accepted?" The Donovans were loyal but unbending people who did not accept help, even when they desperately needed it.

"That's what Rogan said, but still…"

"Why don't you give him a chance? When the time comes, let's look at a few houses and if it feels right, we can make an offer. If not, we'll rent. Tate doesn't seem like the kind of man to push or hold it against you." She hesitated, then let the truth spill out. "From what I can tell, you're the one who holds a grudge and makes judgments, not him."

His hand stilled, and he looked up at her, the brackets around his mouth deepening, his brows pinched together in an expression that said *annoyed and not happy*. "You think so? You think I judge?"

"I think you let your unwillingness to trust get in the way of logic. I understand why you do it because I do it, too. But there comes a time when you have to trust someone, and I think Tate Alexander's a person you can trust." She clutched his hand. "And I think it's time to admit that."

He studied her, lips pulled into a frown. "I see."

Those simple words and the dark expression on his face told her he was pulling away, shutting down right in front of her. "Don't do this, Luke. I love you and I'll go along with whatever you want. I'm only asking you to consider Tate's offer as an option. And while I do think you tend to judge, it's not a criticism. I have my own faults and trust me, I'm not proud of them."

He raised a brow. "Care to share?"

She shook her head, reached out and stroked his jaw. "Not now. Not yet. I'm still working on them."

He turned and kissed the palm of her hand. "Fair enough." He laid his head back on her belly, said in a quiet voice, "Judgmental, huh?"

The anger had shifted. Helena leaned forward, kissed his temple, and murmured, "Maybe a little."

"Yeah, maybe a little."

And just like that they were back on even ground, the conversation switching to the floorboards he'd torn out in Rogan's living and dining room, and the plumber who was working on drain lines for the upstairs bathrooms. Helena listened to him talk about drywall, hard-wood floors, and light fixtures, heard the excitement in his voice. A few weeks ago, she had no idea what a recessed light was let alone that it could be dimmed to completely change the mood in a room. Her world continued to expand, her heart to swell with love for Luke and their baby. He really did seem happy. Content. Maybe this life would be enough for him. She brushed a lock of hair from his fore-head. Maybe it was time to confess.

But then she pictured his expression when he heard she'd been keeping important truths from him, ones he might think questioned his honor and integrity and she couldn't get the words out.

Not yet. Soon.

Hours later, Helena's secrets would be threatened by the one person who'd welcomed her into the family: Rose Donovan. It was a simple request asked with the shyness of one who isn't certain her wish will be granted and yet hopes it will be.

They were finishing a meal of roasted chicken, stuffing, and grilled asparagus, when Luke's mother cleared her throat, set down her fork, and fixed her gaze on Luke and Helena. "I want to ask you both something I've been thinking about since I heard you were married." Her lips pulled into a faint, sad smile. "Jonathan and I talked about the day our children got married, the joy we'd feel—" she sniffed, cleared her throat again "—the beauty and honor of witnessing that moment. He never got to see any of you marry." Her blue gaze turned bright, darted toward the ceiling. "That's not true. He witnessed all of your weddings; I was the one who did not."

Helena clasped her hands together, sipped in tiny breaths, and waited for Luke's mother to make her request. What could she want? *Please do not let it be the one request that will expose what I've done. Please. Not that.*

Of course, it was exactly that. A mother doesn't speak of missing her son's marriage and sprinkle words like *joy, beauty, honor,* and *hope* and not wish for a chance to know it. Rose Donovan's next words spilled over Helena, stole her thoughts, squeezed her chest until it ached.

"Will you renew your vows? Please?"

She could not think, could not feel or process—

"Of course, we will." Luke reached out and stroked Helena's cheek. "We'll be honored to, won't we, babe?" Her head dipped a fraction, not quite a full nod, but enough for him to consider it a yes. "Thank you," he murmured, his voice low, his lips brushing her temple. "I love you." Then he turned back to his mother and said in a voice filled with curiosity and humor. "Sounds like you've given this some thought? Care to provide a script of what you'd like us to say?"

Rose Donovan's expression softened, her eyes turned brighter. "No, dear, I think you'll both know exactly what to say."

Those words and the heartfelt request settled in Helena's brain, made her restless and unable to sleep for the next two nights. Uncertainty and confusion suffocated common sense, made it difficult to consider the possibilities of their situation, or the solution. Would it be so bad if she and Luke exchanged real wedding vows before she was one hundred percent certain he wouldn't tire of marriage and a family? Nothing in life was guaranteed, not even a sure thing or a promise of happily-ever-after. Maybe it was time to trust her instincts and marry him for real, become Mrs. Lucas Donovan: wife, partner, soulmate. Her heart told her he was committed and wanted a life with her and their baby and while it was scary, she would trust her heart.

If she and Luke renewed their vows, vows that weren't legitimate the first time, then they'd be truly married, and he'd never have to know the first wedding wasn't real. Life would begin for them in Reunion Gap, surrounded by his mother and the rest of his family. Yes. *Yes*, she breathed, her soul expanding with love and hope. Once they were married, she would find a way to tell him she owned one third of her family's greeting card company and was the creator of the Annabelle Grace card line. He'd be angry—okay, furious—but she had to tell him before the baby came. Didn't she? She sipped in tiny breaths to calm herself. Of course, she had to tell him; she couldn't go on pretending she'd been near bankruptcy and was hoping to sell one of her cards to the Annabelle Grace line. How could she do that when she *was* Annabelle Grace?

One day, he'd probably have to meet her brother and sister, though there was no rush for that. Who knew what Dominic and Estelle would have to say about Luke, or worse, what Luke might have to say about them? They did not possess the warmth or graciousness of Rose Donovan and to them, family loyalty meant duty to the business. That was another reason she wanted to be part of the Donovan clan; they believed in loyalty and duty to *each other*.

Once Helena reconciled the idea that fate and Rose Donovan had determined it was time for a vow renewal, or in Luke and Helena's case, a real wedding, she wanted to set a date and get married. It sounded so easy and should have been. However, easy often morphs into impossible and three days later as they sat in the mayor's office, Helena realized that's exactly what this situation was. *Impossible.*

Martin Olanski was a big man with a ruddy complexion, a shock of white hair, thin lips, and the darkest eyes she'd ever seen. Hawk eyes that darted over a person, burrowed into their soul to spot a truth from a lie. When he stood to shake hands, those eyes narrowed on her, targeted her belly. "Helena, welcome to Reunion Gap. It's nice to meet the woman who's won this man's heart." His gaze slid to Luke as he clasped his hand, pumped up and down three times. "Nice to see you again, Lucas. It's been much too long."

Red splashed Luke's cheeks and he mumbled, "It's been a while..."

"Have a seat and let's see what we can do to put a smile on your mother's face." Mr. Olanski sank into his chair, folded his hands over his protruding middle and said, "Rose says you want to renew your marriage vows." When Luke nodded, he continued, "Easy enough. I just need to know the where and the when, and I'll be there." He shook his bushy head, let out a laugh. "Hard to believe. Lucas Donovan, a married man."

The tone in Mr. Olanski's voice made Helena wonder if there was more to the man's words than simple statements. It was almost as if they belonged on a billboard—placed in the center of town as a grand announcement for all the females in the area. Luke must have felt the same way because he laced his fingers through hers, squeezed.

The mayor reached for a pen, jotted down a few notes. "We'll set a date once we have a copy of the original marriage certificate—"

"The..." Helena swallowed, tried to clear the buzzing in her head that made it difficult to speak. "Marriage certificate?"

"Right, we'll need that." His voice slid three octaves, took on a conspiratorial tone. "I instituted the policy a few years back when a young couple tried to pull a fast one by telling me they were married when they weren't. All they wanted was the party their parents promised, and I sure caught a lot of grief for not checking." He let out a sigh, rubbed his jaw. "I know you two would never do that, but I can't break the policy." Another sigh. "My secretary would have my hide. Tell you what; how about you give me the information and I'll have her take care of getting the copy?"

How were they going to get a copy when there wasn't one?

"Great, thank you." Luke turned to Helena. "Do you know where we put the marriage papers?" His voice slipped. "Or the name of the guy who married us?"

Yes, she did know. They were tucked away inside one of her notebooks, and how could she forget Sam Henderson, friend and waiter from the restaurant? Helena met Luke's gaze, held it, and offered up one more lie in a string of several. "I'm not sure. I'll see if I can find them, okay?"

Luke nodded, turned back to the mayor of Reunion Gap. "We'll locate the information and get it to you as soon as we can." He stood, extended a hand. "Thanks for your help, Mr. Olanski. You're going to make my mother the happiest woman walking this earth."

HARRISON ALEXANDER never accepted no as an answer unless he was the one saying it. He'd learned from his father that acting as though you were in charge was the first step toward *being* in charge. It didn't matter if the issue wasn't his business; what mattered was his *interest in making it his business.*

There'd only been one time in his life where someone told him no and he'd been unable to reverse the decision. Rose Donovan had turned down his offers and professions of love, and it hadn't mattered that he'd wanted to go against his father's wishes and break his engagement to a wealthy southern socialite. Rose hadn't wanted him or his promises.

Her rejection had made him bitter and determined to destroy the man she'd chosen over him. For years he'd held onto the hope that one day she would come to him and admit she'd never stopped loving him. But she hadn't done that. No, damn it, she'd stood before him as venomous words shot from her mouth. *Jonathan Donovan owned my heart from the moment I first met him. And you? You were a mistake I have spent every breathing moment trying to forget.* Harrison sipped his coffee and thought of Rose and her perfection: the sky-blue eyes, high cheekbones, slender neck. And oh, the luxuriousness of her silky hair...

His recent illness had forced him to realize he might not have decades left on this earth; he might only have years, or months. That didn't sit well with a man who controlled life and the people in it. He sure as hell expected to be around a lot longer than a few months or a few years and if he could increase his chances with those damnable heart-healthy meals, exercise, and cutting back on the alcohol, then he'd do it because before he took his last breath, Rose Donovan *was* going to admit she cared about him and that "no" she'd flung at him would become a "yes."

That was his long-range plan, but he had several short-term agendas that required his attention, beginning with his brother's disastrous personal situation. He'd invited Camille for coffee, but his sister-in-law wasn't fool enough to believe this was a social gathering. No, she was much too smart to think him interested in benign conversation that did nothing to move his plan forward. Camille had always been the one who could read a room and anticipate the outcome of a conversation long before the last words were spoken. Carter possessed the IQ to soar through medical school and every other academic venture he pursued, but he did not have the patience or the interest to understand people or what motivated them.

And that made him ineffective and weak. It also made his estranged wife a powerful opponent. Camille sat across from Harrison in his study, sipping a fresh-ground coffee blend that reminded him of a brew he'd once sampled in Italy. Dark, rich, robust, more memorable and more enticing than his companion had been.

"Excellent coffee, Harrison." Camille offered him a faint smile, her petite frame swallowed by the leather couch. "But we both know you didn't invite me so I could compliment your coffee selection." A tilt of her head, followed by a small laugh. "Let's get this over with, shall we?"

Harrison settled in his chair and prepared for the cerebral sparring.

Carter was such a fool. Camille was a breath of intelligence, beauty, and determination, and if her husband had stopped chasing every woman with a heartbeat, he might have seen that, and his life wouldn't be a mess right now. Still, there was time to make amends and ask forgiveness, and if Harrison provided the handbook, Carter need only follow the play-by-play instructions for a chance to save his marriage. The big three on the list that could not be altered or erased were the essential ones: give up the pregnant girlfriend, keep his zipper shut, pay attention to his wife. Were they really so difficult? Harrison let out a long sigh, worked up a smile. "You know me well, Camille."

"Oh, I doubt that, but I know your *tendencies*." She laughed again. "Probably as well as I know your brother's."

"Ah, yes, my brother." He reached for his coffee cup. "He's a fool to let you go, and I believe he's finally realized that."

"Why do you say that?" She raised a brow, her blue eyes narrowed on him. "Because I spoke with him the other day and while he said all the right words and even put feeling in them, he doesn't want to be with me any more than I want to be with him." Camille fingered the rim of her coffee cup, said in a soft voice laced with steel, "The charade's over, Harrison. You can't keep saving Carter from his mistakes. Let him fall once or twice and maybe he'll grow up and accept his responsibilities, like doing right by the pregnant girlfriend."

"You can't be serious." He sucked in a breath, forced himself to remain calm. "The girl's barely out of high school. The father's a drunk, the mother's a runaround...and there's a litter of siblings who may or may not share the same father." He sighed his disgust. "You think I'm going to have *that* tied to the Alexander name?" He shook his head, eyed her. "Absolutely not, and if you believe for a second I'll permit it, then you have not been paying attention."

Carter's wife set her cup on the coffee table, cleared her throat. "I don't see where it's your business, unless he's asked you to make it your business." She paused, crossed a silk-clad leg over the other and continued. "I don't need a list to know you've bailed him out more than once, which is why you think you have a right to say what happens to him. That may be true and if that's how he chooses to live his life, so be it. But *I* choose to live my life a different way, not for him, not for you, not for anyone."

The woman had grit and fire, he'd give her that. "There isn't going to be a divorce, Camille. You and Carter *are* going to work out your differences and go on as you always have. Life isn't about getting what you want or chasing happiness. Haven't you realized that by now?" She could still have a good life, all she had to do was agree to stay married and Harrison would see to it his brother curtailed his extracurricular activities. No more skirt chasing, no more carousing at night. Nothing but dedication to his career and the woman he'd married thirty years ago. Carter would agree because Harrison would leave him no choice.

"You think that's how this is going to play out?" Those tiny nostrils flared, the eyes flashed, the complexion matched her red hair. "I've ignored my husband's philandering for too many years because I loved him and was foolish enough to believe he cared for me, too. I thought if I could be everything for him he wouldn't need to look elsewhere, but guess what? That man is unable to think about anything but his next conquest. Now he's got someone pregnant." Her voice dipped, and she looked away for the briefest of seconds before she swung her gaze back to burn him with a fierceness that almost made *him* look away.

"Stop playing with people's lives, Harrison. Haven't you learned anything from all those hours in the hospital? You can't manipulate people or situations without consequences, and you should have learned that by now." A rushed breath followed by more accusations. "Your son isn't talking to you, you've been tossed out as CEO of your own company, and you're more miserable than you were before the stroke."

What to say to that? Harrison sat up straight, clutched the armrest of his chair and homed in on his target. "I did *not* have a stroke. It was a transient ischemic attack, otherwise known as a TIA, and I'm stronger and better than ever." He jabbed a finger against his chest, forced a smile. "Healthy eating, exercise, a commitment to stress reduction, and an increase in mental stimulation." The smile inched wider. "Never better." He liked Camille, but she'd crossed the line with her bold-faced comments.

"Good for you. Then since your mental capacity isn't in question, I'll reiterate: *leave your family alone*. All of them, including Carter. They don't need or want your involvement, and I won't sit by and let you try to stop this divorce." She grabbed her handbag, stood. "Why do you have to be like this? There's a coldness in you that you can't blame on birth or family. Did someone hurt you long ago? Is that why you're determined to make the rest of the world suffer? Because *you* aren't happy? Well, I'm not going to sit by and watch you destroy any more lives—especially mine."

"Marriage is a vow and you can't just extricate yourself from it when it's not convenient for you anymore."

"Are you serious?" Her cheeks burst with red, her words singed with anger. "What about all of your mistresses? Did you honor *your* vows?" When he didn't respond, she went on. "No, not a single time, did you? Poor Marguerite had to sit by and suffer through the humiliation. Oh, I know all about being humiliated."

"I run this town, Camille, whether you care to acknowledge it or not." Surely, she understood the power he wielded, power he could use for or against her at any moment he chose—to do anything he chose. Money was a great motivator; it attracted the weak, the desperate, and the greedy and could gain all manner of assistance. Hadn't he employed that strategy against his nemesis Jonathan Donovan, Camille's do-good brother, when he'd manipulated Gordon T. Haywood to destroy the man? What would Camille say if she knew Harrison was behind that scheme? If Donovan had been a worthy opponent of strong character, he would have found a way to survive. Harrison would have cut him down again, but the man would not have fallen on his sword after the first skirmish.

Now he was gone, and Rose Donovan was within touching distance.

She didn't know it yet, but he *would* have her.

And perhaps Camille could help. He would have to think on this and determine her usefulness.

Harrison stood, smiled, and offered his hand. Camille stared at the gesture, ignored it. "Leave us alone. I mean it, Harrison."

"You know I can't do that, Camille." His smile widened, but his hand fell to his side. "It's not in my nature to sit by and watch things flounder. I prefer to jump in and take care of the situation." A pause, a raised brow. "Sometimes I even choose to put them out of their misery."

Chapter 11

There came a time in a man's life where he had to stop thinking about pride and payback and just suck it up and do what needed doing. That didn't mean it would be easy or that he wouldn't rather down three shots first or hurl accusations and condemnations in one final stand of protest, but then what? He'd still have to do the deed because this wasn't about him anymore. It was about the woman who owned his heart and the baby she carried—his baby. Their family.

Luke sucked in a breath and entered HA Properties, Inc. Talk about high-end. The mahogany furniture in the reception area, the glass tables, the fresh-cut flowers, the paintings. How did a person work in a place like this? Did he take off his shoes so he didn't drag in mud? Oh, right. People like Tate Alexander didn't know what mud looked like. *Crap, cool it. You need a favor from the guy and you can't go in all pissed off.* Luke approached the receptionist desk where a woman who looked around his mother's age smiled at him.

"Mr. Donovan?"

He nodded. "Yes, ma'am. I'm here to see Tate Alexander."

The smile spread, warmed her brown eyes. "He's expecting you."

Luke shrugged out of his jacket and followed the woman,

surprised Alexander hadn't chosen eye candy for the front desk position. A man selected that type for the way she looked and the way she made him look. Alexander didn't mind his wife working in a factory, wearing jeans with holes in them, and steel-toed boots, so maybe he wasn't into eye candy. Not that Charlotte wasn't good-looking because she was, but once that mouth got started, a man couldn't get lost in the green eyes and curves or she'd swallow him up whole.

"Luke. Nice to see you." Tate Alexander moved toward him, shook his hand.

Yeah, like they hadn't just seen each other in his mother's kitchen this morning. Who knew Alexander liked peanut butter and banana sandwiches for breakfast? "Hey. Thanks for fitting me in."

"Sure."

He motioned for Luke to sit and eased into the chair next to him—not the big-ass leather one behind the big-ass desk. Luke cleared his throat. "So..."

Alexander crossed a leg over his thigh, fiddled with a tassel on his fancy loafer. "You know you didn't have to schedule an appointment."

Luke homed in on the loafers. He'd bet they were Italian. And the socks? Who wore striped socks? Damn, but he did not want to have this conversation with Pretty Boy. Thoughts of Helena floated through his brain, snuffed out his dread. "I know, but this is business."

"Right, but you're family." The man paused, said in a quiet voice, "Or maybe I should say *I'm* family now. You could have talked to me one of the several times we run into each other throughout the course of a day." Another pause, followed by a faint smile. "You know, the times we're trying to avoid each other."

Had the guy just admitted he'd been avoiding *him?* Damn, but he had. That made Luke grin. "Yeah, I'm aware of those."

"Unfortunately, so is your sister, and don't think she doesn't critique every slight and let me hear about it." He let out a long sigh, played with the tassel on his shoe. "Thanks for bringing turmoil to my marriage and for being the reason my honeymoon to Hawaii got postponed."

There was a hint of humor and something else in the man's voice. Annoyance? Yep, the tone and the pinched lips said the guy was ticked. Luke shrugged, crossed his arms over his chest. "Don't blame me if you can't keep your wife happy." He raised a brow, continued with the jab, "And if she doesn't want to honeymoon in Hawaii with you, well, I guess that says a lot, doesn't it?"

Tate Alexander sat up, gripped the arms of his chair, and burned him with that silver gaze. "Trust me, I have no problem keeping my wife happy. You, on the other hand, have her so worried she doesn't want to get on a plane and fly thousands of miles away until she knows you're..." He paused, rubbed his jaw. "What was the word she used? *Stable*. Yes, until you're stable."

"Stable? What the hell does that mean?" What the hell *did* that mean? Did his sister think he was a nut case? Mentally imbalanced?

A shrug, followed by a thin smile. "You tell me. I'm not the one she thinks is unstable." He toyed with the loafer tassel, let more sarcasm drip out. "Maybe she's worried your bride will see you for the reckless, irresponsible fool you are and run back to Colorado."

"Shut up. Helena's not going anywhere." Alexander was the fool. Helena wasn't going anywhere; why would she when they'd planned a life together here in Reunion Gap? She was carrying his baby and they were renewing their marriage vows. Did that sound like a person about to bail? No, it did not. Still, the man's words unsettled him. "I'm not the same person I was the last time I left town. I've changed." He glared at Alexander, bit out, "And I'm not going to do anything that could jeopardize my marriage. I came here to ask for your help, but I should have known better." He stood, grabbed his jacket, and hurled a parting blow. "How about we keep avoiding each other like we've been doing? That worked just fine with me, and maybe you'll hurry up and build your palace, so you can get the hell out of my mother's house."

He'd made it five steps before Tate called him. "Hey."

Luke swung around, fists clenched. He couldn't wait to get out of this place, back to fresh air and trees. "What?"

Alexander stood, moved toward him. When he was an arm's length away, he stopped. "I'm sorry; I was out of line." The brackets around his mouth deepened. "But comments about my marriage, even as a joke, are off limits."

Damn but the guy was touchy. He guessed he understood because Luke didn't like references to his being unstable, reckless, or irresponsible. And he definitely did not want to hear insinuations that once Helena knew the real Luke Donovan, she'd hightail it back to Colorado. "Got it."

A nod and then "Okay, so let's try this again. How about we sit down and have a real conversation, minus the jabs? I'm up for it if you are."

That was it? Rogan would never move on without blistering Luke with a lecture on responsibility and common sense. "Sure." He was not going to wait for the guy to change his mind and start the lecture. "And, sorry about the comments."

Tate Alexander studied him a second too long before he opened his mouth and said, "Thanks." The mood shifted and he smiled. "You've got a very protective sister...in case you didn't know."

Luke shook his head, sighed. "Tell me about it. You'd think I was the baby in the family. I'm not a complete idiot." His lips twitched, and he hid a smile. "At least not most of the time."

"Are you going to ask me to keep whatever we discuss a secret?" Alexander's expression turned grim. "Charlotte and I don't keep secrets so that could be a problem."

Damn, but the guy really did love her. Tate Alexander might have caused Luke a ton of aggravation in the past, much of it created by Luke's distaste for the wealthy and their privileges, but he might have to reconsider his initial assumption and admit the guy was a decent human being. He was still a Pretty Boy, but he was a decent one who loved his wife. Yeah, Alexander would get extra credit on that last one. "You can tell her. She'll be proud of me once she gets over the shock." Luke laughed, tossed his jacket over the back of his chair, and sat down. "First, I don't want you to think you have to say yes because you're married to my sister. This has nothing to do with that."

"Fine."

"I love my mother, but Helena and I need a place of our own. We want to hang on until the baby comes, save up some money, and see what we can find." He rubbed his forehead, slid a glance at Tate. "Rogan said you have rentals and some real estate and maybe we should talk to you."

Tate stared at him. "That's it? You want to check out real estate options?"

Heat surged from Luke's neck to his cheeks. "Pretty much." He couldn't get a read on the guy. Was he insulted? Ticked? What did that stare mean? Seconds ticked by without a response. Too long for a person like Luke. "Look, maybe I shouldn't have come. It's no big—"

"Of course, it's a big deal or you wouldn't have made a point of seeing me at the office. I give you a lot of credit because asking me for *anything* had to be tough, even though I already offered my help."

Where was he going with this? Luke might have to reconsider downgrading his opinion of the guy if he were setting Luke up for a grand smackdown. "Right." Another five seconds and Luke would gather his tattered pride and leave. Five, four, three, two—

"You must really love her."

Those silver eyes narrowed like they could see right into his brain. "I do love her." He wasn't ashamed to admit it, or what he'd do for her. "And I'll do anything for her and the baby. It's not about me anymore; it hasn't been since I met Helena."

His brother-in-law's expression softened, his lips pulled into a faint smile. "Yeah, I figured as much. I'll get the specs on the houses available to rent and buy and give you the name of our property manager. She can show you whatever you like." His voice shifted, filled with emotion. "Pick out what you want. If you decide to buy, I'll make sure you get a great deal."

"I don't expect you to do that." All he wanted was a little direction...

Tate met his gaze, held it. "I never knew the meaning of a real family until I joined yours. It's the least I can do." Those eyes grew brighter, glittered. "We're family, Luke, and family takes care of its own. Please, let me do this."

AFTER, Luke would wonder if the disaster that became his life might have been avoided if he'd skipped his aunt's house and headed straight home. He'd been anxious to tell Helena about his meeting with Tate. She'd be happy to hear he'd sought out his brother-in-law and asked for his help, especially since she knew the man wasn't among his top ten favorite people. Not even top one hundred. But that opinion had changed since their conversation and it had nothing to do with the man's offer to give him a great deal on a house. No, Luke's changed opinion had to do with Tate Alexander's desire to be part of the Donovan family and what could only be described as true compassion.

He and Helena had talked about renting until they could afford a home of their own, but maybe with Tate's offer, they'd be able to buy sooner. A year ago, he hadn't been interested in renting a place longer than a few months. *Keep moving* had been his motto. *Don't stop, don't slow down, and don't look back.*

All that changed the day Helena Montrey walked into his life with a bowl of hot-and-sour soup and an egg roll. Who would have thought he'd be thinking about a home, a real home with mail delivered to Mr. and Mrs. Lucas Donovan? He smiled, hopped out of his truck, and bounded up the front steps of his aunt's home. Who would have thought...?

Luke rang Camille's doorbell, waited for someone to answer. His aunt's home was a smaller version of the Alexander mansion, from the outside anyway. He couldn't compare the inside since he'd never been in the Alexander mansion, though he could guess. But after his conversation with Tate this afternoon, he had a new respect for the guy and the fact that blood relations didn't make a family, no matter how much money they had.

The door opened and a tall man in a dark suit ushered him in. Growing up, Luke had visited his aunt's house a handful of times. It was one thing to laugh and enjoy Camille's company in the Donovans' living room, and quite another to witness her transformation once she crossed the threshold of the home she shared with Carter and their children. Spoiled brats, including the husband. Luke wouldn't have come today if Camille hadn't left him three messages saying she had to see him ASAP. He sighed at his aunt's tendency toward the dramatic, handed the butler his jacket, and followed him to the "sitting" room. He remembered this place because it was covered in chrome, glass, and cherry—not intended for children.

"Mrs. Alexander will join you in a moment."

The dark suit bowed and disappeared, leaving Luke to contemplate whether the British accent was real or the result of practice. Who knew? This place made him jumpy and he'd dreaded the few times he'd had to come. No matter how much he wanted to have a good time, something bad always happened when he came here. He glanced at the Oriental rug and wondered if it were the same one he'd puked on when he'd eaten too many jelly beans. Or if Carter had ever found out Luke had broken one of his favorite vases. It was a clean break and Camille made sure it got fixed, but Luke knew the damn thing cost more than his father made in a month.

He'd never been able to draw a clean breath in this place for fear he'd puke or break something again. Bad things happened when he visited this house and while he wasn't a kid any longer, bad things could still happen.

"Lucas!" Camille descended upon him in a fluff of pale blue, her high heels clickety-clacking toward him. "Dear boy, it's always lovely to see you."

She flung her arms around his neck, hugged him tight, then pulled back. Next came the kiss on the cheek, followed by a brush of her fingers to remove the lipstick mark she'd left. Luke grinned down at the tiny woman who never seemed to run out of energy—or lipstick. Some things never changed. "You just saw me four days ago." He let out a laugh and added, "And aren't you coming to dinner tomorrow night?" Maybe she was too lonely in this big empty house that had become more mausoleum than mansion with the kids and the husband gone.

Her blue eyes misted, and her smile faded. "This couldn't wait." She linked her arm through his and pointed to the couch. "Let's sit."

He didn't like the tone in her voice that said bad news was headed his way. And what about the tears? Not good. "Did something happen to one of the kids?" Luke had never been a big fan of his cousins, but maybe they'd grown up and weren't the spoiled brats he remembered. People changed. Look at him. He wasn't the same angry, self-destructive, reckless jerk he'd been the last time he left town.

"No, Victoria and Simon are fine." She eased onto the couch, patted his arm. "I wish Oliver were here. I miss him so. He's always such a calming force." Pause, a sniff. "But when your best friend tells you he's got stage four pancreatic cancer, you don't ask him to hold on a few months while you spend time with your family. I doubt he'll return from California before Donnie passes."

Donnie had been lead vocals in Oliver's band and his best friend for longer than Luke had been alive. "I'm anxious for Oliver and Helena to meet, but it can wait; we're not going anywhere."

"Actually, the reason I called you here is because of your *wife*..."

"What about her?" Why would she want to talk to him about Helena? Camille had only met her a few times and as far as he could remember, they'd seemed to like one another. Yes, his aunt had been inquisitive, but so what? That was the Donovan way: ask questions, then ask more questions.

"Well..." She drew in a breath as though capturing enough air for the words that would follow. "A few months ago, I became acquainted with a private investigator from New York. He was trying to locate the whereabouts of his friend's daughter. The woman had disappeared over ten years ago with a man—" she clutched his hand, squeezed "—

and the mother had no idea what had become of her. That's when Lester got involved. Lester Conroy is Texas born and bred: a real cowboy type with the Stetson, boots, big belt buckle, and a nose for tracking. His investigating led him to believe the woman might be in Reunion Gap." Her voice dipped, swirled around him like she was telling a story that was not part of someone's life. "Of course, you can't send a lanky cowboy with a drawl into our town and not rouse suspicion." She cocked her head to the side, whispered, "That's where I came in. Lester contacted me because of my association with the town and asked me to do a little digging and report back to him."

Luke stared at his aunt. "He asked you to 'do a little digging and report back,' as in spying?" *What did any of this have to do with Helena?*

She nodded her red head. "Yes, and he said I was very good at it. He called me a natural."

"I see. So, did you identify the woman? Was she in Reunion Gap?" Maybe she hadn't wanted to be found; had anyone ever considered *that*? He didn't care about the woman who didn't want to be found; he only cared about whatever his aunt had to say about Helena. But knowing Camille, he wouldn't find out until she'd told the rest of this convoluted story.

"We did identify her. It was Jennifer Merrick."

Jennifer Merrick? "You mean the woman who owns the bed-and-breakfast?"

"The very same one." A faint smile hovered about her lips. "She's since reunited with her mother, who had no idea she also had a granddaughter. You remember little Hope, the shy child who rarely speaks?" When Luke nodded, she continued, "They've already visited each other once and I believe they're heading back to Jennifer's hometown again soon. And at some point, the mother is coming here. Plus—" she leaned in, patted his hand "—your Uncle Oliver is sweet on Jennifer. She's sweet on him, too, but it's all hush-hush for now."

"Yeah, I get it. He's trying to protect the poor woman from the Donovan interrogation routine." Helena had been great about his family's mountain of questions, but he could tell there were times when it bothered her. "So, are we done with the private investigator story? I need to get home, and you said you had something to tell me about Helena."

"Yes." She cleared her throat, those blue eyes settling on him. "Yes, I do. Have you ever heard of the Annabelle Grace greeting cards? There are a few different lines: Annabelle Grace Loves, Annabelle Grace Lives, Annabelle Grace Laughs, and Annabelle Grace Cries."

He raised a brow, stared. "Everybody's heard of them, especially the sticky-sweet love cards." Heat swirled to his face, settled on his cheeks. "I've even been known to buy one or two." A shrug, followed by a throat clearing. "Helena likes them. She's written a few samples for the company and is waiting to hear back. Why do you ask?" Why did his aunt care about those cards? Had Helena shared her hopes to write for the company? She was private about it, but maybe Camille had said something that made her share.

"I ask because...because Helena writes these cards."

Why did his aunt look so miserable? So, they weren't literary masterpieces? Who cared? She was writing about feelings and emotions and people could relate. "I know she writes these cards. I just told you that." He rubbed his jaw, sat up straight and checked his watch.

"No, Lucas. Helena writes cards for the company and has been since the beginning."

"The beginning of what?"

She blinked, blinked again. "The beginning of the Annabelle Grace line. Helena *is* Annabelle Grace."

"What?" He squinted at her as though he couldn't comprehend the meaning behind her words, which he couldn't because none of it made any sense. "Helena's Annabelle Grace?"

Camille's head dipped. "Yes," she murmured.

"Helena's Annabelle Grace," he repeated. "Then she's not just a waitress...not almost bankrupt." Luke paused. "She's...she's..."

"Wealthier than I am? Part owner of a major greeting card company? The creator of a very successful greeting card line?" She laid a hand on his forearm, "Yes, to all of them."

"But..."

"Why didn't she tell you? Why did she keep it all a secret? I have no idea and neither does Lester."

"Lester? The cowboy investigator?" When his aunt nodded, Luke stood, shoved his hands in his back pockets to keep from punching something. "I don't believe it. The guy's either lying or there's a mistake."

His aunt folded her hands in her lap, glanced up at him. "Lester Conroy is an honest and decent man who wouldn't lie. And there's no mistake. I have the report to prove it."

"Let me see it. I want to read the accusations with my own eyes and then—"

"He's not lying, Lucas. I have photos, too. It's the truth."

"Truth? You want to talk to me about truth? Let me see the report." He paced the room, sucked in air as the oxygen in the room shrank. There was a mistake, *there had to be.* He'd finally gotten his life together, was happy and in love, married, for hell's sake, and expecting a baby. This could *not* be happening.

"There's more."

Luke swung around, faced his aunt. "More? How much more could there be than this Lester's accusation that Helena is some rich greeting card princess? This is crazy. My wife would not have lied to me, not about something like this." Maybe his aunt was used to a husband and wife lying to each other, but Luke and Helena had vowed to always tell the truth. No matter what. They were a team. But his aunt's next words told him how wrong he'd been—about everything.

"She's not your wife. The marriage isn't real."

Chapter 12

Helena spent the early afternoon helping Rose bake pumpkin pies. *The trick is in the fresh nutmeg*, she'd said, *and not overbaking. Too many people follow recipes step by step instead of trusting their gut and using common sense. If an oven runs hot, then adjust your cooking time. If your husband prefers extra cinnamon, don't be afraid to add a pinch more than the recipe says. Adapt, that's what life is all about, just like marriage.* Her laughter had trickled from the kitchen sink to the table where Helena stirred the pumpkin into a large mixing bowl.

Life was settling down and she and Luke had started talking about a place to live that was not the house where he'd grown up. Maybe one of these days Luke would look past his old prejudices toward Tate Alexander and talk to the man about their housing situation. Luke was a strong-headed, proud man who didn't want to owe anyone, but maybe he'd admit they could use help and a little direction, and Tate could give them both. Some nights, Luke pulled out a notebook and showed her the plans for his dream house: a two-story log cabin. *One day, I'll build it for you*, he promised. *And it will have everything in it we want.* When she'd tried to tell him all she wanted was him, he'd laugh and kiss her. *You'll always have me*, he said. *No matter what.*

What he should have said was *You'll always have me. Until I find out the truth you've been hiding.*

"Helena?" Rose disrupted her thoughts, pulled her back to the present. "Once we finish the pies, why don't you rest a bit and I'll make us a cup of tea?"

Since they'd arrived in Reunion Gap, the woman had been working her way down a list of her son's favorites that included homemade applesauce, fried chicken, wedding soup, meatloaf and mashed potatoes with garlic and sour cream. The pies were for tomorrow's "Thanksgiving" dinner because Luke had missed it and, according to Rose Donovan, this family had a lot to be thankful for, especially new members and upcoming babies.

How to argue with that? Helena wasn't used to family meals or traditions and the very idea that Luke's mother cared enough to create several meals for her son despite the work and time required was heartwarming. "I'll fix the tea," Helena said. "Chamomile?"

Rose nodded her dark head, her blue eyes sparkling. "Tate brought me a tin of macarons; they came straight from some fancy store in New York. We'll sample those, too."

"I'll never turn down a macaron." Helena added the remaining ingredients to the pumpkin mixture, plus an extra pinch of cinnamon —because Luke loved cinnamon—and turned off the mixer. She was about to ask Rose for the next step when the front door banged open, followed by footsteps and Luke's voice—loud, angry, uncontrolled.

"Where is she?" He stormed into the kitchen, homed in on Helena who stood with a spatula in one hand and his mother's recipe in the other.

"Luke? What's wrong? What happened?" But the look on his face said he was in no mood for questions.

"We need to talk." He pointed a finger to the hallway and the direction of their bedroom. "Now."

"Lucas?" His mother wiped her hands on a dishtowel, moved toward him. "Settle down. You look dreadful. Let me get you a glass of—"

"Mom, I don't want anything except the truth, and you can't help me with that." His gaze narrowed on Helena, burned into her. "You, on the other hand, can. Let's go."

Helena placed the recipe on the counter and the spatula in the empty pumpkin can. "Rose, would you mind finishing?" She didn't wait for an answer but turned and followed Luke from the room. Of all the ways she'd pictured this moment playing out, this had not been it. In fact, she'd been certain she'd be the one doing the telling—when the time came. But somewhere between her first lie and now, he'd uncovered his own version of the truth and it didn't match hers. He motioned toward the bedroom, waited for her to enter before he followed and slammed the door shut.

"Damn you." He shrugged out of his jacket, tossed it on a chair. "Was this all a joke?"

"What? No, no. Luke." She moved toward him, but he held up both hands to keep her away.

"Stay right there. I don't want anything from you but answers. Can we try that and this time, let's go for the truth?"

Helena sank onto the edge of the bed, clenched her hands into fists, waited. Maybe it wasn't as bad as she thought. After all, who would have told him anything? "You're making me nervous."

That brought out a harsh laugh. "Good one. I'm making *you* nervous. Is that how you get guys to stop asking questions? That's called *deflection* and I'm the king." He leaned against the dresser, crossed his arms over his chest, and said nothing. If he were trying to intimidate her, then he was doing a darn good job. Helena cleared her throat, waited. It didn't take long for him to lodge the first attack. "You're rich. Filthy rich. Sick rich. Annabelle Grace greeting cards? That's your family." He shook his head, sucked in a deep breath. "*That's you.* And here I was trying to build up your confidence to submit more work. I'm such a fool and you played me all the way."

Nothing she said now would make a difference, but she had to try and explain her reasons for keeping her identity a secret. "I had to make sure you cared about me and not...my money."

"Your money?" He stared at her like she'd just said she had to make sure he wasn't a monkey. "Are you serious?"

"People do it all the time." Pause, a swipe at her cheeks. "It happens."

"Did you ever care about *me* or was it just a game, a lie and a way to pass time?"

The disgust on his face was not that of the man who'd laid his head on her belly and talked to their baby or promised to build her a log cabin one day. That man was gone, killed by her dishonesty, and he wasn't coming back. A stranger had taken his place, cold and unforgiving. "Luke, please..."

"Please? Please what? Please understand I've been lying to you from the second we first met? Please understand it was nothing *personal*? Or please understand that I didn't trust you enough to tell you the truth, not even when you were spilling your guts to me?" He cursed under his breath. "Take your pick. Any one of those," he spat out. "Or all of them."

"I never expected to meet anyone like you but then you walked into my life, big and bold and beyond anything I could have imagined. I was scared. I'd *never* felt that way before and I wanted to trust you, but how could I after I'd been betrayed?"

"Huh. So, another guy burns you and the next one has to pay the price?"

The look he gave her said it was a poor excuse and he wasn't buying it. "It sounds horrible when you say it that way, but—"

"But? But it didn't matter because it was all about you? You didn't mind screwing me over while you were screwing me? Tell me, Helena, because I want to know why you would torch what we had because you were scared."

"I'm sorry." She blinked hard. "I'm sorry," she said again.

"Sorry? That's not going to do it. What other tricks do you have hidden? Because if you're not telling me everything, you can damn well rest assured I'll find out, and when I do, it's not going to be good." She opened her mouth, closed it. "Trying to figure out a lie before you speak again? I wouldn't advise it. Tell me now, damn it, what else did you leave out of our grand romance? Did you target me? Was it fun? Did you and your rich friends laugh at me, see who could nail the unsuspecting idiot and make him fall in love with you?"

"No! No, that's not what happened. I fell in love with you… *I love you*, Luke, and nobody pushed me or told me to do anything. For once in my life, I listened to myself and did what my heart said. And I let myself fall in love with you."

The laughter that fell from his mouth was cold, harsh, brittle. "You *let* yourself fall in love with me? Well now, don't I feel special?" He closed the distance between them until he was a touch away. "Do you know how many women would have done anything to hear an 'I love you' from me? To get a commitment and a damn ring?" He eyed the ring on her left hand, let out another laugh, this one colder, harsher, more brittle than the last. "The ring. What a joke! I thought I was buying you something that was beautiful and elegant, worthy of our love. Were you laughing at me because it wasn't two carats or were you laughing because I was a fool?"

"Neither." She clasped her hands together, held them against her belly and their unborn child.

"There might be a lot I don't know about you, but there's more you're not telling me. I couldn't see it before because I refused to look and didn't want to hear it from my siblings, but now I'm watching you with eyes wide open. I'm listening, too, and what I'm hearing is a lot of silence between the words. What are you leaving out, Helena? And remember, if I'm asking, I already know."

"We're not really married," she blurted out. Helena would remember the exact moment his love died; his expression turned dark, his lips thinned, his gaze narrowed, and then his features relaxed and evened out—to nothing.

"Not. Really. Married. Huh." He rubbed his jaw, said in a flat voice. "That's what I heard."

"Everything happened so fast...and then I found out I was pregnant."

"Yeah, then you found out you were pregnant."

"And you pushed marriage."

"*I* pushed marriage?"

He didn't like that. "You wanted to get married. I thought we should wait..."

Luke stared at her. "I wanted to get married because I loved you and we were having a baby. I thought we were starting a life together and I wanted to do it the right way."

"The right way?" A slow burn started in her belly, worked its way to her throat. "You admitted to your restless, wandering past and I was supposed to jump up and down that for a nanosecond you wanted to marry me? I had to be sure you weren't going to feel trapped six days, six months, or six years later."

The lack of emotion evaporated, and he exploded with a string of curses, each more colorful than the last. "How'd you do it? Who was the guy you paid to fake the wedding?"

She looked away. "He worked at the restaurant with me."

He blew out a long breath. "I see."

"Luke, I'm so sorry." Helena stood, took a step toward him. "I did it for you. I wanted to make it easier...if you changed your mind."

"Nice. If I changed my mind. You think I'm so unreliable I would ditch you and the baby?" Her hesitation made him scowl. "Of course you do. Why wouldn't you after I spit out all that touchy-feely garbage about getting restless if I were in one place too long and not knowing what I wanted to do with the rest of my life? Add that to my whining about never measuring up to my perfect brother and that doesn't sound like a guy I'd depend on either." The scowl deepened, spread across his face. "Most guys are full of insecurities, but they keep them buried so they can appear in charge and tough. Until a woman comes along who *insists* he's got to spill his guts to bond and whatever other crap she says is necessary for a relationship. I'm the fool for trusting you when all the while you were sitting back and taking notes...and judging."

"I never judged you or thought less of you." How could he say that? She'd *wanted* him to share, had felt so close after he'd admitted the parts of his life that weren't so great or that he wished were different. Yes, she should have done the same instead of glossing over details and changing facts, but there'd been her identity to protect. "It takes a strong person to admit life isn't what he wants it to be."

"Yeah, strong and stupid." He scratched his jaw, studied her. "You weren't stupid, though, were you? You played the innocent: shy, alluring, so damned tempting." Those pale blue eyes glittered. "I doubt any man could resist that combination. I know I couldn't, but then I've never been known for my restraint, especially where a beautiful woman was concerned." His voice turned soft, mesmerizing, "I was so sure you were different, so sure you'd made *me* different, but it was all a joke."

"Please don't say that."

"Why? You faked our marriage." He shook his head, cursed under his breath. "What else did you fake?" His gaze slid to her belly. "Is this baby really mine?" His voice turned hoarse. "Or am I just the fall guy?" Helena gasped but before she could respond, he went on. "Hear me out. Considering your backstory and the lies you've told, it's possible I'm not the father, but a convenient fill-in. It makes sense if you think about it. We landed in bed days after we met, something you swore you'd never done before. I believed you because I wanted to, even though a tiny piece of me wondered how a 'good girl' could be so damn passionate. But what if you weren't a good girl and the fast track into bed wasn't your first time? What if there was a reason to get me into that bed and into the relationship?" Luke paused, homed in on her belly. "Like a baby on the way?"

Okay, now he was being ridiculous, and he was making her furious. "Are you trying to be cruel or do you really believe what you're saying?" She planted her hands on her hips, moved toward him. "I went to bed with you way too soon and I knew it, but I couldn't seem to stop myself. It never happened before and while I'm sure you can't claim the same, I can." Helena took another step toward him, her breath falling out in uneven huffs. "And I don't know what constitutes a 'good girl' but lying in bed like a corpse is not it. The passion came when we were together, and you can deny it all you want, but you know it was there."

The glare said he knew it and didn't like it. "What's your point?"

"My point? This baby's yours and you know *that*, too."

She waited for him to deny it, expected that he would, but all he said was "I wish I'd never met you."

That hurt more than questioning whether the baby was his. Pain shot through her, sucked the air from her lungs. Helena stepped back, away from Luke Donovan and his cruel words. The man knew how to deliver a blow and where to strike to achieve maximum damage.

"I see." She squared her shoulders, refused to let the tears fall. He'd been the one person in her life she'd believed truly cared about her, and maybe he had...maybe beneath the pain and anger, he still did. But in her world when someone attacked, she shut down and went into self-preservation mode.

"When will you tell your family?" It had to be done, and the sooner the better. She liked the Donovans, especially Rose. Elizabeth was sweet; so was Rogan. Tate Alexander acted like he knew all about being an outsider and he'd seemed as eager as she was to be included. His wife was another story. Charlotte had a sharp tongue and a protective air that said she didn't like strangers who couldn't be vetted—like Helena.

And then there was Camille Alexander. The woman was cunning, sophisticated, and saw way more than Helena wanted her to see. She might smile and compliment, but those blue eyes assessed, analyzed, and dissected the details most people missed. She unsettled Helena, despite Luke's belief that his aunt was a softy.

There was nothing soft about that woman.

"Luke? Can I just talk to your mother before you tell her?" She clutched her hands against her belly, forced out the words. "She's been very kind to me and I'd like to say goodbye."

"Goodbye?" He moved toward her, stopped when he was close enough to touch her. "There's no goodbye, not when you're carrying my baby." His gaze slid to her rounded belly, inched to her face. "We're definitely *not* going to tell my mother, not yet. She's had her share of sadness and we're not going to add to it or push her over the edge." His voice dipped. "She wouldn't do well with the news and I'm not having that on my conscience."

"We have to tell her." Didn't he see that it would only be worse to carry on the charade? "It's not fair to let her think everything's fine when it's not."

"How do you know what's fair?" he lashed out. "Fair is telling the truth and being honest when it counts. This—" he thrust a hand in the air "—the pretending we're going to have to do from now on—that's a result of your lies."

Helena looked away, stared at his booted feet. She remembered the first time he removed his boots and she noticed the worn socks and how she'd ordered him ten pairs the next day. He wore the new socks now, padded in the heel with a gray toe. "We can't live like this."

"People do it all the time."

She dragged her gaze to his, took in the harsh lines around his mouth, the stern look. "I can't." How could he expect her to pretend nothing was wrong, that he didn't despise her or what she'd done? "I don't think you can, either," she said in a soft voice.

A flicker of what looked like pain flitted across his face but was gone before she could identify it. "It doesn't really matter what I can or can't do. I *have* to do it. My mother needs to hang onto her belief that after years of screw-ups, her wayward son is finally settled. Boy, wouldn't she be surprised to learn this is the biggest screw-up of my life?" Of course, he didn't wait for her to answer but plowed on. "You owe her, Helena. That woman trusted you and if she goes off the deep end, it's on you. So, until this baby comes and she can hold it in her arms, we're going to pretend we still care about each other. After that, who the hell knows?" Those blue eyes burned her. "But you'd better get used to Reunion Gap because I'm not going to be a long-distance dad." His next words squeezed the air from the room. "And I will fight you for that right, no matter what it takes."

Chapter 13

L uke had suffered his share of black eyes, bruised ribs, cut lips, and bloody knuckles, usually involving another man's fist and too much booze. But the pain he suffered now had nothing to do with alcohol or a bad punch, unless you counted the one his "wife" had landed on him. Oh yeah, she'd done it up right and he'd never seen it coming.

He'd explained the yelling stampede into the kitchen as too little sleep and a misunderstanding with Helena. His mother hadn't questioned him or asked for details, but then Rose Donovan never did, especially when Luke was involved. She may have suspected there was more to the story than what he admitted to over the years, though she never said. His father, however, got the full details and scrubbed part of the truth, like an erased computer hard drive. *Don't admit to anything until she asks, and then wait for her to tell you what she wants to know*, his father had said. Or, *You can tell your mother about the drinking but not the police...*

It wasn't that his father was trying to be deceitful, but the man needed to protect his wife because she didn't do well with too much reality, especially the unpleasant kind. There'd been times when Luke just wanted to get the whole story out and be done with it so he didn't have to worry about keeping everything straight. But the look on his mother's face said *fragile* and comments like *you're such a good boy* and *I'm glad it was nothing worse than that because I don't think I could take it* told him she wasn't in any shape to hear the truth.

That's why Luke knew she couldn't find out about this latest mess, the worst betrayal of his life and one that would destroy her. He wouldn't be responsible for that, not after all the grief and aggravation he'd caused her: the years away, the sporadic visits, the reckless behavior, deserting her when she'd needed him most. It didn't matter that his heart had been ripped open and his soul shredded. All that mattered was keeping the secret safe and his mother happy. She needed something to look forward to and this baby was that something. Sure, Rogan and Elizabeth would give her a grandchild, too, but how many times had she told Luke that his child was his redemption?

Damn it all! Why did Helena have to be a lie?

He might be able to keep the secret about him and Helena from his mother but the only way to do that was to admit the truth to his brother and sister. There was no way around it and while he hated having the conversation, he needed their help. That's why, after a pot roast dinner where his mother chatted away about teaching Helena to crochet afghans and baby booties, he pecked Rose on the cheek, darted a glance at Helena, and said he had to visit Rogan about the next house project.

When he arrived at his brother's, he didn't even have time to shrug out of his jacket before Charlotte was on him. "What's going on? Is something wrong with the baby? Is Helena okay?"

His sister would never make a poker player, not with those emotions, though she did seem calmer since her new husband was in the picture. Who would've ever thought Tate Alexander would be a welcome addition to the Donovan clan? Not Luke, that was damn sure, but a person could only deny the truth for so long. The guy was good for Charlotte. They were in love, happy, parents of Winston the golden retriever, and owners of a soon-to-be-under-construction mini-mansion they would one day fill with little Alexanders.

Life was good.

Luke tried for a smile, failed. "How about a beer and then I'll tell you all about it?"

He followed Charlotte into the kitchen where Rogan sat at the table, obviously waiting for him. A beer rested near his right hand, a frown on his face. Typical Rogan, waiting to pounce, accuse, and offer advice.

Charlotte pulled two beers from the fridge, handed him one, and motioned to the seat next to Rogan. She sank onto the chair opposite her oldest brother, let out a sigh. "Okay. Spill."

He sat down, twisted the cap off his beer, and took a long pull. "There's no good way to say this…"

"What's wrong?" Rogan's voice held an edge to it, reminiscent of the old days. "What did you do now?"

Luke let out a laugh. "Yeah, you mean what did the screw-up do now? Because it's always me, isn't it? I'm the one responsible for every disaster in my life, right? What if I told you it wasn't me this time, that I've been blindsided by Helena?" He took another pull on his beer, wished it were his third so the words would grow hazy, the feelings inside them hazier still. He did not want to feel pain. He did not want to feel *anything*.

"I'd say I want to hear about it." Rogan's gaze narrowed on him. "And I'd say I want the whole story from the beginning, not the version you think I want to hear."

Charlotte grabbed Luke's hand, squeezed. "Luke? What are you talking about? What about Helena?"

He rubbed his eyes, blinked. "It's a freaking train wreck and I'm the one caught under the tracks."

"English, please?" She squeezed his hand again. "No more metaphors."

"Camille called me to her house this afternoon, said it was urgent. You both know how I hate going there, but I went." He placed his left hand on the table, zeroed in on the gold wedding band. Yeah, what a joke. Mr. and Mrs. Lucas Donovan. "She told me about this investigator guy she knew and how she hired him to find out more about Helena. I wanted to be pissed that she'd do that, but the look on her face told me the guy found out something I wasn't going to like."

"And?" Charlotte leaned toward him, brows pinched together.

She'd always stuck up for him and tried to protect him—when they weren't arguing. "I found out Helena isn't who she says she is. She's rich, greeting-card-heiress rich, and here I thought she was almost bankrupt." A cold laugh, followed by a curse. "That's what she told me, so why wouldn't I believe her? I mean, when you're all-in, you don't lie to each other, do you?"

Charlotte shook her head, said in a quiet voice, "No, you don't."

"I promised to save her from financial ruin, imagine that? Me, the King of Debt Disaster, promised to fix things." He'd been an idiot *and* a fool.

"Why wouldn't she tell you the truth?" Rogan's gaze narrowed on him. "Was it a test? Was she trying to see if you loved her for herself and not her money?" He scratched his jaw. "I don't like the why, but it would make sense."

Luke blew out a disgusted sigh. "Yeah, I guess that would make sense. That's what she said anyway. She told me after the last disaster with a fiancé who was after her money, she had to be sure I wasn't another hunter. Like I ever cared about money. The woman made me look like an idiot and I was pissed off, but I guess I could have found my way around it, eventually."

"But?" Charlotte's question held a mix of sympathy and dread.

"But it was about a whole lot more than a single lie." He studied his beer, brought it to his lips, and finished it off. Then he set it on the table and dragged both hands over his face.

"What happened?" Rogan fiddled with his beer bottle, shot him a look that said *this better be the truth.*

"I guess it's payback for all the times I was less than truthful, but man, this was a torch job. I know you and Elizabeth had your issues —" he looked at Charlotte, forced a smile "— and you and that husband of yours had a detour or two, but I think this one beats both of those. Helena let me believe she was all-in, encouraged me to spell out way too much this-is-how-I-feel crap, which I did because I believed it's what you did in a relationship. Like I really ever knew what one of those looked like. But how the hell do you have a relationship with somebody who lies about her identity?" Luke sucked in a breath, blew it out. "I thought she was different; I thought she was the one person in my messed-up world I could count on, the one I could build a life with that mattered." He looked away. "It was all just a bunch of BS. After she gutted me, I wondered if the kid was even mine but the look on her face told me it was, but who really knows? I mean, do you ever really know what's real?"

"Luke, talk to us." His sister's voice turned soft. "Tell us what happened."

"Tell you what happened?" he said, surprised his heart could still beat. "A disaster happened. A tsunami." Pause, a deep breath and a whoosh of air from his lungs pushing out the horrible truth. "She faked our marriage. Imagine that? She friggin' faked our marriage. And do you know why? She said she wanted to give me a way out in case I got restless and wanted to bail on her and the kid. Nice, huh?"

"Damn." This from Rogan followed by another, "Damn. I guess maybe I could kind of see her point but that's rough."

"You can kind of see her point?" Charlotte scowled at Rogan. "What kind of person does that? I don't buy it… I don't buy anything that woman says."

Well, reference to Helena had shifted to *that woman*. That was never good in his family. When references to *that woman* started, it meant his siblings were gunning for the person and it wasn't going to be good. Family protected family, and the Donovans protected their own even if they didn't agree with them. Helena had no idea what was in store for her, not with Charlotte making statements like she just had and referring to her as *that woman*.

Rogan sipped his beer, eyed Luke. "I don't know what to think. Logic says she could be telling the truth… Or she could have faked the marriage to protect her assets if things go south."

Luke slapped the kitchen table with the palm of his hand. "I never thought of that one. She's got a hell of a lot of assets to protect; maybe that's it. Maybe it was never about me at all."

LUKE OPENED the bedroom door and slipped inside. The soft glow of the nightlight illuminated a corner of the bed. He eased out of his work boots and socks, unbuckled his belt, and stepped out of his jeans. The long-sleeved flannel shirt came next, leaving him in a T-shirt and boxers. He kicked them into a pile against the dresser and made his way to the bed.

She lay on her side with her back to him, long hair spread on the pillow. He knew the silkiness of that hair, the coconut smell, the way it tickled his chest when she moved over him. How many nights had they lain in each other's arms talking about the future, their baby, their dreams? So many plans and all of them filled with hope and promise and the absolute knowing it would happen.

And now it was all over. And it had all been a lie.

He should not be surprised that she'd manufactured such emotion. It's what she did for a friggin' living. Their relationship had consisted of *I love you* and *I want to spend the rest of my life with you* and *we will grow and learn and thrive together*. There'd been other phrases, ones meant to tug at his soul and make his heart swell. The woman was a master at creating emotion, and she'd created enough feeling in him to make him believe in happily-ever-after. But once he'd learned the truth about her, the emotion had shifted from joy and love to disgust and anger.

Helena Montrey had stolen his heart and ground it up.

Luke squinted, let his gaze follow the lines of the comforter, take in each curve... He knew them all so well. Had touched, tasted, kissed every one of those curves and now all he wanted to do was block them from his memory and pretend none of it had ever happened. How in the hell was he going to do that? The damn woman lived inside him and the only way he would survive this betrayal was to learn to hate her.

He eased a pillow from the bed, grabbed the afghan resting on the back of a chair, and tossed them on the rug before he slid to the floor and yanked the afghan over his body. Tomorrow he'd wake up sore and stiff, a reminder that he wasn't twenty anymore. Still, anything was better than sleeping in the same bed as the woman who'd broken his heart.

Luke woke an hour before his usual time, scrubbed a hand over his face and yawned. A glance at the bed told him *she'd* turned on her side, arms outstretched in the space where he usually slept. A pang of something he refused to identify as compassion shot through him seconds before he snuffed it out, grabbed his clothes, and headed for the shower. Life would go on and they *would* get through this...his mother would not find out the truth... When the time came to offer her a version of what had happened, it would be reworked, massaged, and manipulated so as not to be identifiable. It would be palatable, though, and as his father had taught his kids, that's what their mother needed: a reworked story, not the hard and often cruel truth.

Fifteen minutes later, he bounded down the steps and made his way to the kitchen. His mother sat at the table, sipping coffee and paging through a cooking magazine. "Hello, dear, you're up early today. Is everything all right?"

No, Mom, everything is not all right. In fact, everything is all wrong. Of course, he couldn't say that, so he forced a smile, gave his mother a peck on the cheek, and said, "Never better. Crazy day and I want to get started."

"I understand your brother's keeping you very busy. I'm so happy you two are getting along so well."

"Yeah, just dandy." For once his know-it-all brother wasn't the problem. Unfortunately, the woman he thought was his wife, the one who was carrying his baby, *was* the problem. He reached for a mug, poured coffee into it, thought of how Helena used to bring it to him in bed when they were still in Colorado. *I thought you should be served in bed*, she'd said with a soft smile. *You certainly worked hard last night*. Her cheeks would turn red, her eyes bright. He'd glance at her half-naked body, murmur, *I did work hard, didn't I?* And then he'd set the coffee aside and show her just how grateful he was for her services.

"Lucas? Would you freshen up my coffee?"

He blinked, carried the pot to the table, and refilled his mother's cup.

Sleep had eluded him last night, his brain bombarded with questions and concerns about how they were all going to keep the disaster that had become his life a secret. And what about the damn marriage vow renewal? What were they going to do about that? Knowing the mayor and his stickler tendencies, he wouldn't go for anything that looked suspicious even if he'd known the Donovan clan most of their lives. Luke would talk to Rogan and see if he had an idea about how to get past this. Or maybe Tate would know. The guy might be a do-gooder, but his father was a shyster and a double-dealer and maybe some of those genes had rubbed off—for emergency purposes only.

But there was another problem that was more long-term, more painful. How was he going to look at Helena and pretend they hadn't shared hopes of a life and a future? And that body? Did he really think he could blink and erase the memories? He was a fool, but even he wasn't that big a fool.

"… and I thought Helena and I would work on making a cake from scratch today. I told her how much you love carrot cake and she wants to make it for your birthday. Oh, I know it's not for another two months, but still…she wants the practice." She smiled, flipped a page of the magazine. "She's such a lovely young girl. Wants to please you so much; it does my heart good to see how much she cares about you." Her voice dipped, turned soft and sad. "Your father would be overjoyed to know that his children were all settled and some of them were welcoming the next line of Donovans. I wouldn't be surprised if Charlotte didn't turn up pregnant in the next year. I've seen the way her husband listens when you all talk about babies and pregnancies.

Men ignore those sorts of details until they're interested in becoming a father themselves. Imagine three little Donovans all living in the same town, playing together, going to the same school…"

Yeah, imagine one of those little Donovans where the mother lives in one house and the father lives in the other. "It's nice to dream, Mom, but don't turn the dreams into fairy tales. Real life happens, even to the best of us."

"Dreams are meant to be lived and fairy tales are meant to be created." Her blue eyes grew wistful. "Your father and I had such dreams and we were so happy, but it just wasn't long enough. Does that mean I wish I'd never had that joy or known that love?" She shook her head, clasped her coffee cup between her hands. "No, of course not. Besides, your father lives in my heart and my soul and he will never leave me."

Luke had to look away from the sadness and pain on her face. *That's* what real love looked like. That's what family and hope and sacrifice were all about. "I wish things could have been different for you, Mom."

"Whenever you open your heart to love, you also open it to pain. Remember that, Lucas, especially when life gets difficult."

What to say to that? Fortunately, Luke didn't need a response because his sister took that exact moment to barrel into the kitchen with Winston close behind. Leave it to a dog to lighten the mood. Charlotte rushed to him, hugged him tight, and whispered, "How are you?"

"Okay." That wasn't the truth, but he figured she didn't expect the truth, not with their mother sitting a few feet away.

"Tate will be down in a minute so I'm going to take Winston outside." She darted a glance at their mother, smiled. "Hi, Mom. Say good morning to your first grandson."

Rose laughed. "Who would have thought I'd call a dog my grand-child?" Her voice turned gentle, her lips pulled into a smile. "He's my buddy. I don't even want to think about the day you all move out. I'm just hoping you'll take trips, so I can babysit him."

"If Tate has his way, he'll be flying me all over the country. And you know he's building you a mother-in-law suite." Charlotte leaned down, rubbed Winston's ears. "Did you hear about that, Luke?"

"A mother-in-law suite?" Luke glanced from Charlotte to his mother. "Guess somebody forgot to tell me." Tate Alexander was building their mother her own suite in his mini-mansion? Charlotte hadn't said *she* was the one doing it, which he found very interesting.

Rose laughed and lifted her coffee cup to salute them both. "At least my son-in-law looks out for me. He's mentioned Winston might want a brother or sister, and someone else for me to babysit." She tilted her head, studied Charlotte. "What I can't figure out is if he's talking about a four-legged sibling or a two-legged one."

"A two-legged what?" The subject of their conversation walked into the kitchen. "Why is everybody looking at me?"

His wife leaned on tiptoe, whispered in his ear. He laughed, said in a voice filled with humor and gentleness. "I'm talking about a dog, Rose. When I'm talking about a baby, I think Charlotte should be the first one to know, don't you?"

Luke thought about his sister and her husband as he worked at Rogan's that day. He was glad they'd found each other, gotten through their differences, and were making a life together. Marriage was a damn crapshoot and it wasn't easy. He'd never been interested in it, had been determined to remain unattached and uninvolved. But then *she'd* come along and changed his mind. Not that she'd had to work very hard to change his mind because there was something about her that made him *want* to reconsider his position on permanent bachelorhood. He'd been a fool to think *he* was the one making the choice when it had been her all along.

Chapter 14

"How could you?" Anger and disgust spilled from Charlotte's lips, spread through Rogan and Elizabeth Donovan's living room. "Don't you know what you've done?"

Helena swiped at her eyes. How could there be more tears after yesterday? Luke's words singed her brain. *I was so sure you were different, so sure you'd made me different, but it was all a joke...I wish I'd never met you...* She and Luke were over, done, their hearts and hopes crushed, and she was responsible for all of it. "I never meant to hurt him. I would never do that." She forced out a truth Luke's sister might not want to hear. "I love him."

Charlotte balled her hands into fists, burned Helena with those green eyes. *"Love?* What do you know about love? Do you have any idea what my brother has done for you? He's *never* brought a girl home, never introduced us to anyone, and there've been a lot of women. Luke's not the kind to open up and share, but he said you were different; he called you an angel who'd been sent to save him from himself." Her laughter spun around the room, changed to a snarl. "But you're no angel, are you? No, you're the she-devil who betrayed him."

"Charlotte." Elizabeth laid a hand on her sister-in-law's arm.

"Why don't we listen to what Helena has to say so we can understand what happened?"

"What are we going to understand? Will she tell us how my brother got played? How she ripped his heart apart and left him to bleed out?" She glared at Helena, spat out, "Are you really pregnant? And if you are, is the baby Luke's?"

"Of course, it's his. I would never…"

Those green eyes turned to slits. "Yeah, right. You would never… Everybody says that, until they do."

Elizabeth became the mediator once again. "Charlotte, we've all done things we wish we hadn't. Sometimes we do them because we're afraid of getting hurt or afraid to trust. And sometimes we do them for reasons even we don't understand. Let's give Helena a chance like people gave us a chance."

"It is not the same. No way."

"Yes, in some ways it's exactly the same; we just don't like to admit it."

What were they talking about? Helena couldn't imagine Elizabeth doing anything wrong. As for Charlotte… Well, she could definitely see where Luke's sister had a temper *and* a tendency to get into *situations* of her own making.

Charlotte blinked hard, the left side of her jaw twitching. "Did you see Luke's face? He'll never recover… Never trust anyone again." Her voice cracked, shook with anger and sadness. "We've lost him, and we'd only just found him. He'll leave." More anger, piled on top of sadness. "You'll see, and we'll never be able to find him again."

"You don't know that." Elizabeth touched Charlotte's arm, offered a smile. "Let's sit down and listen, okay? And try to keep an open mind. It wasn't that long ago that both of us were on the outs with our men, and no matter how much we don't want to admit it, we were the cause."

"That's not exactly—"

"Yes, it is, and we both know it." Elizabeth patted a spot on the couch next to her. "Now sit and don't talk until Helena is finished." A mumble and a curse escaped Charlotte's lips before she crossed her arms over her chest and fixed her gaze on the floor. "Go ahead," Elizabeth said, her voice soft and persuasive, so unlike her sister-in-law's. "Help us to understand."

What did any of it matter now? There was no sense trying to protect her pride or her privacy when it was obvious she'd lost both. Helena perched on the edge of the rocker, studied the wood trim Luke had replaced last week. He was talented and kind and—

"Well? We're waiting."

Helena met Charlotte's gaze, held it. "I was sixteen when my mother died. My father had passed away five years earlier, so when Mom died, it was just me and my two siblings. We had money, lots of it, but we didn't have family to care about us or guide us. That's what the lawyers and trustees were for, I guess." She shrugged, looked away as memories of the early days without her mother clogged her brain, burned her heart. "We'd always hung around the company; it's what made us feel closest to our parents." Pause. "My brother and sister were older and already in college. Once they finished, they took over the business and marketing departments." Her voice dipped with remembering. "I became the creative director when my sister found the stacks of cards I'd written to mourn my mother's death. She said I'd found my calling, but I always thought it was just a way to honor my mother."

"So, you wrote sympathy cards?"

Helena sighed, glanced at Elizabeth. "That's how it started out. When you're a child and you're lost, you try to find an anchor somewhere. Anywhere. The sympathy cards were my anchor back then until I fell for a philosophy major my freshman year in college. He used to quote Democritus and Aristotle, and I could hardly breathe when he was near. I was sure I was in love, even though I'd never spoken a word to him and I'm certain he didn't know I existed. That's when I replaced the sympathy cards with love and forever ones. I'd stay up at night writing them and they became so popular my brother and sister talked me into transferring closer to home sophomore year."

She paused, rubbed her temples. "That way I could commute and produce more work."

"But what about your studies and enjoying college life?"

It was easier to focus on Elizabeth and her concern and pretend Charlotte weren't there. Rogan's wife had a softness about her that said she cared and understood. Charlotte, on the other hand, did not seem to possess that same softness or interest in anything Helena had to say. "There was too much money involved. The cards sold well and the people they hired to replicate the work couldn't get the same feel."

Elizabeth frowned. "Did you mind transferring?"

Helena opened her mouth to spit out phrases like *My brother and sister needed me*, and *I wanted to help out*, or even, *I had a gift and I had to give back—for my parents*, but she couldn't do it. Not this time. If they wanted the truth, she'd give it to them. "Yes, I hated it. I didn't want to write cards. Not then, maybe later, after college, but not when I was twenty years old. I did what they wanted, though; I transferred and had to settle for average grades because I spent so much time creating cards about love and soulmates. Meanwhile, I lost my time, my freedom, my friends." Her voice wobbled, cracked. "I lost my choice."

Charlotte snaked her a look, gaze narrowed, watchful. "I'd be pissed."

Elizabeth had a gentler response. "I'd be torn. I'd want to stand up for myself and follow my heart, but I'd probably let guilt creep in." Her amber eyes turned bright. "And the desire not to disappoint. I know what that's like."

"I guess I do, too," Charlotte said. "It's no fun being the only girl, especially with a perfect oldest brother like mine. At least Luke and I were on even ground with the screw-ups, but I get it. You don't always want to be the odd one out. You want to do something that makes someone proud." Her tone shifted from understanding to unhappy. "But that didn't mean it was okay to lie to my brother."

Helena shouldn't have lied to Luke or pretended who she really was, but she'd needed to be sure Luke cared about *her* and not the assets attached to her name. "I never wanted to hurt him. If you believe nothing else, please believe that." She sucked in a deep breath, forced out the memory she'd tried to bury. "I was engaged and about to marry when the man I thought I'd spend the rest of my life with admitted he loved someone else. Oh, he said he still loved me, but in a different way." She paused, let the pain seep through her words. "But *she* was the one he wanted to marry. Not me. I didn't understand until he started talking about finances. You see, I'd put his name on my house, bought him a car, given him money. We were going to be married soon enough; what did any of it matter?" She swiped at a tear. "But it did matter. A lot. And it cost me. I even had the privilege of paying for a wedding that never happened."

"Bastard," Charlotte hissed.

Elizabeth shook her head. "That's horrible."

Helena clasped her hands in her lap, stared at the clenched fingers. "I withdrew after that. How could I trust any man when I couldn't trust my judgment to pick a decent one? I sold the house and told my brother and sister I couldn't live near any reminders of what had happened. They didn't like it, but they didn't have much choice, not if they wanted my work. That's when I started drifting from town to town, picking up odd jobs, trying to fit in and create. It was the creating that saved me. There was so much pain and anger inside, I had to get it out." She let out a quiet laugh, shrugged. "Once the Annabelle Grace Lives cards hit the shelves, they skyrocketed. Guess I wasn't the only miserable person who'd been done wrong."

"And then Luke came along?"

Charlotte's tone had turned more curious and less confrontational. Helena nodded. "I wasn't interested in getting involved with any man, certainly not someone like your brother."

"Like my brother?" The raised brow and clipped voice marked her displeasure.

Helena met her gaze. "A man who knows how to make a woman feel like she's the only one who exists."

"Ah." It was Charlotte's turn to nod. "My brothers both have that skill...so does my husband."

It was difficult to tell whether that was a compliment or not. Elizabeth was much easier to read than Luke's sister, and she didn't shoot the evil eye whenever she didn't like a response. Still, how could Helena fault the woman for caring so much about her brother and trying to protect him? "But I never felt like I was being played or that his intentions weren't genuine. I knew the signs from my last relationship disaster and Luke told me how his friends' wives tried to match him up, and how it always ended in a mess. We were honest about our feelings for one another, even when those feelings scared us because they were too soon or too strong."

Elizabeth nibbled on her bottom lip, her hand resting on her pregnant belly. "But you didn't trust him enough to tell him who you really were?"

"It wasn't Luke I was worried about; it was me. I didn't trust myself to be objective where he was concerned. When he was around, the emotions were so high and strong, I couldn't think." Her voice dipped, softened with remembering. "I worried that I'd grow desperate enough to settle for anything, and I couldn't do that. I had to know he cared about *me*, not the money. And when I found out I was pregnant, and he wanted to get married, I couldn't go through with that either..."

"You know women usually have a fake pregnancy, not a fake marriage," Charlotte said with a scowl.

Helena ignored the comment. "I was *not* going to trap Luke into a marriage he'd later regret. I wanted to give him time to see what it would be like once the newness of us being together wore off and the baby came along. I figured if he still felt the same way, then I'd convince him to have a more formal ceremony—a real one."

"And you'd never tell him how you'd tricked him into thinking the first one was the real one?" Charlotte jumped off the couch, paced the room, hands fisted on her hips. "You think it's okay to just lie in a marriage?"

"No, of course not." Helena clutched the edges of the chair, sucked in deep breaths. She loved Luke; she'd done this for him. *Couldn't anybody see that?*

"I'll bet you almost croaked when Mom suggested you renew your vows." Charlotte shook her head, continued the pacing. "Though I have no idea how we're going to tell her about you and Luke..."

"We're not." Elizabeth glanced at Charlotte, then settled her gaze on Helena. "We're not going to tell Rose because that poor woman has nothing to hold onto but the happiness of her children. Rogan thinks she's slipping again and he's worried about her. He said we should all act like everything's fine with Luke and Helena, and I agree."

"But what about the ceremony she's organizing? We can't go through with that." Luke hadn't spoken a word to her in three days, had disappeared for hours and taken to sleeping in Rogan's old room, telling his mother Helena couldn't get comfortable in the tiny bed. As if they hadn't fallen asleep on her couch more than once and slept all night. But he'd spoken with such sincerity, why wouldn't his mother believe him? Why wouldn't anyone believe the man when he looked at them like that, when the words that slipped from those lips were coated with caring and concern?

"She's right," Charlotte said from across the room where she was doing yoga poses. "This would be a real ceremony with the mayor officiating. Mr. Pomp and Circumstance is definitely going to require a copy of your marriage certificate." Pause as she moved into a downward dog pose. "And since you don't have one of those..."

Elizabeth rubbed her belly as though the baby inside would soothe her. "Oh, this is not going to be easy."

"The mayor did say he needed a copy of the certificate. He offered to have his clerk request a copy if we provided the details." Helena rubbed her temples, remembering the conversation too well. "Of course, there are no details to provide..."

"Since there's no marriage certificate," Charlotte said, then added, "At least not a real one. I suppose you could create a fake document."

Elizabeth sighed. "Charlotte, I'm going to pretend you didn't say that. We'll find a way; it's just going to take some creative brainstorming."

"Uh-huh." Charlotte crouched on the floor, did a handstand against the wall. "Good luck with that."

What a mess. No amount of clever brainstorming would guarantee Luke would show up for a ceremony—even if it were fake—where she was the other half of the couple. Helena placed a hand on her belly and thought of the baby. What did she know about being a mother? People said you learned as you went along, that you did the best you could and that's all anyone expected. But what did that really mean? That no matter what you did, you'd probably mess up your child in some way so just accept it? What if the parent were the mess? What if she weren't fit to be a parent?

And what about Luke? He'd admitted being a parent hadn't been on his radar. Yes, *radar* had been the word he'd used, but then he'd smiled and said something like *every good pilot knows how to change course when necessary.* She'd been so caught up in that smile and the huskiness in his voice that she hadn't dissected the meaning in those words. And when his tanned fingers splayed across her belly, there'd been no room for logic *or* common sense. Emotion took over and she let herself believe they could be a couple, could be parents, could have a life together. She let herself believe withholding the truth was protecting them both until they were sure, but all it had done was destroy what they'd shared.

"I don't want to hurt anybody else," Helena said. "I'll do whatever this family thinks is best."

Charlotte kicked out a leg and ended in a standing position. "That's the best idea I've heard since you arrived."

Elizabeth ignored Charlotte. "Don't give up. I know it seems hopeless right now, but please, don't give up on Luke." Her next words spilled with sadness and understanding, "And don't give up on yourself. I'll help you. I'll come to your doctor appointments if you want, be by your side as long as I can..." She smiled, let out a soft laugh. "Until this baby decides to join us."

This woman was goodness and compassion and Helena would need that in the coming months. "Thank you." She spotted Charlotte approaching her, tensed for the woman's next comments. They would be harsh and judgmental, like a sister protecting her brother. How could anyone fault her for caring so much? But when she spoke, there was curiosity rather than condemnation in her voice.

"Why would you stay? Even if you figure out a way around the marriage thing, then what? Do you know how difficult it's going to be for all of us to see my brother and pretend you're still a couple? And what about you?" She tucked a lock of hair behind her ear, those green eyes narrowed on Helena. "Luke is less forgiving than I am, and way less trusting. I know my brother. Even if he still cared about you, he'd never admit it, not even to himself. I agree that we can't let Mom know yet, but down the road, after the 'marriage,' if that happens, you two are going to have to move on."

Move on. What did that mean? And how did a person move on when she couldn't imagine life without the man who owned her heart? Was it even possible? Tears slipped down her cheeks, trailed to her chin, landed on her shirt. She would need to be strong for the baby, find her focus and direction, with or without Luke, but not today. That time would come soon enough. Helena opened her mouth to answer Charlotte, but all that fell out were whimpers.

"Oh, Helena." Elizabeth scooted off the couch, hugged her. "We'll figure this out. Don't give up yet. Please."

More tears followed by shoulder heaving and gushes of torment. "I'm so scared." Pause. "And so sorry. So sorry." For a short time, she'd believed she'd be part of this family, share the holidays and the dinners, learn the recipes and the stories that made the Donovans who they were. Most of all, she'd *belong*; people would care about her for herself, not for what she could do or what she could buy them. Luke had promised to teach her how to foxtrot and waltz and he'd laughed when she told him she had no rhythm. *I'll teach you,* he'd said. *We'll be great together, you'll see. We're naturals.* But there would be no dancing or finding anything out together because she'd ruined that chance the first time she lied to him. "I love him," she whispered. "How can I move on from that?"

"Hey." Charlotte laid a hand on Helena's shoulder, said in a gentle voice, "I may not be your biggest fan, but if my brother really loves you, the truth will sneak out one way or another. We just have to be looking for it." She leaned down, whispered, "And if we see it, we won't stop until we make sure he sees it, too."

Chapter 15

Enough was enough. How long was this craziness between Luke and Helena going to continue before somebody with a logical brain stepped in and put a stop to it? Those two cared about each other; it was obvious to anyone within eyeshot of them. Well, it wouldn't be obvious these past few days because they weren't speaking much and made a point not to look at each other unless Rose was in the room.

Poor Rose. She had no idea her son and the woman she thought was his wife were suffering right now. Nope. Rose Donovan was so busy planning a wedding vow renewal for the unhappy couple that she failed to notice how miserable and uncoupled they were. When Charlotte filled Tate in on the rest of Helena's story the other night, she'd talked about a user ex-fiancé and siblings who cared more about their sister's greeting card production than her. His wife had used words like *sad*, *tragic*, and *hopeless*, and he'd seen the gleam in her eye that said she might have misjudged her almost sister-in-law and intended to do something about it.

Tate couldn't leave his wife to devise a plan on her own, not unless he tempered her overimaginative ideas with a few common-sense ones—which he would provide once he had more information.

That's why he'd invited Helena to the office and he guessed she'd accepted because she realized Luke wasn't going to talk to her. About anything. That wasn't exactly correct. Tate had the unfortunate bad luck to overhear a few snippets of conversation between them last night.

Luke? Can't we try to talk?

It's too late for talking.

Don't do this. Please.

I've got nothing to say to you.

I love you.

Stop it. Don't you dare say that again.

Tate had closed the bedroom door, glad Charlotte hadn't heard them. That's when he'd decided something had to be done about this standoff and invited Helena to the office. She sat on the couch a few feet away, looking sad and so alone. He couldn't think of her as a Donovan because she wasn't really married to Luke, even though Rose still thought they were. It was a mess, maybe as bad or worse than the disaster he and Charlotte had faced. Who could say? When lies and subterfuge got in the way of honesty, it was never good. People got hurt, hearts were shattered, lives destroyed, even if the intentions were honorable. *Had* Helena's intentions been honorable? That was the big question and one he intended to find out.

"I know you're hurting," he said in a gentle voice. "So is Luke, even though he'll never admit it. If you still love him and want to be with him, then whatever you can tell me will help."

She sat on the other end of the leather couch, her amber eyes sparkling with tears, her voice smothered in sadness. "Love him? I love him so much it hurts to breathe. I can't imagine life without him. I know I made mistakes, hid the truth from him when I shouldn't have... I'm so sorry, but it doesn't matter. He refuses to talk about it." She sniffed, cleared her throat. "He'll never trust me again and I don't blame him, but all I want is another chance and I'll do anything to get that."

Tate rubbed his jaw, tried to determine the sincerity of her words.

The tears were real, though most women could manufacture them on command. But the emotion, the rawness in her voice, the desperation on her face? That told of pain and tragedy, the kind that came from love gone wrong. He sucked in a breath, blew it out long and slow, anticipating the second his next words registered. "Charlotte told me you're not really married."

She blinked, blinked again. "Oh. Yes, of course she'd tell you. That's what husbands and wives do, right? They tell each other the truth." Her voice dipped, filled with sadness. "I wish I'd gone through with the wedding… The real wedding. I didn't want to tie him down; I wanted to give him a choice and a way out if he changed his mind." A shrug, followed by more words coated in sadness. "That was foolish of me, wasn't it? I should have married him and then he might have to try and work things out and couldn't get rid of me so easily." Pause, and then, "Rose is pushing the vow renewal and I'm worried about what will happen to her if we don't go through with it. Luke said her mental state is frail and I don't know what she'll do if she finds out we were never married."

That was everyone's worry. What would happen when Rose found out the marriage was just a sham? Would she suffer another break-down? Would she give up? Would she feel so betrayed she'd fall into a deep depression? Again? "Everyone's worried about that, especially Luke." Rogan and Charlotte had tried to ask him about the vow renewals and what he planned to do, but he'd said he couldn't think about it. For a shoot-from-the-hip kind of guy like Luke Donovan, that meant there might still be hope. "If he hasn't told his mother the truth about you and him, then there's still a chance he'll go through with it."

"You mean he'd marry me for real to save his mother? He'd *never* do that." When Tate nodded, her shoulders slumped, her voice cracked, "I don't know if I could survive that, but what about Rose? I can't be responsible for her heartache."

"Yeah, that's pretty much how everybody feels. If you're exposed, then what? Rose is supposed to forget the hours in the kitchen with you, the handkerchief wedding things she's teaching you to make? And what about the stories she's shared because she believes you're family?" He did not want to think about the betrayal his mother-in-law would feel. "She's come to love you, Helena, and she believes you're the perfect match for her wayward son. You don't steal that from a mother and tell her it was all a lie."

Helena sat up straight, clasped her hands against her knees and murmured, "It wasn't a lie, Tate. The emotions were real." Those eyes that reminded him of a bourbon neat glittered. "We *were* good together." Her voice dipped as though there wasn't enough oxygen to get the words out. "He wouldn't have hurt me; I see that now."

Why did people always see the truth when it was too late? If Helena had trusted Luke enough to be up front with him from the beginning, the guy might not have liked the fact that she had money, but he wouldn't have bailed on her. And the fake wedding would have been a real wedding, no doubt about that. Tate had seen the way Luke treated his "wife," like a man who's been gifted a present he thinks was meant for someone else—because it was too good to be true. He knew that feeling; that's how he'd felt about Charlotte; that's how he still felt. But he'd also known the hurt and anger of betrayal when she'd gone behind his back and confronted Marybeth Caruthers and asked the woman if her son was his. That still stung when he thought about it, which he tried not to do.

Helena's actions were inexcusable and wrong, but he could see why she wanted to protect herself and maybe protect Luke, too. Of course, Luke would never see it that way, not when he'd finally gotten the courage to care about a woman. Tate understood that, too. "Look," he said, "I get what you did, and I even understand why you did it. Charlotte and I have had our own trust issues and the whole not-wanting-to-open-up-and-get-hurt thing. It wasn't good, and we got past it, but not without a little—" he rubbed his jaw, worked up a smile "—family interference."

Her face paled. "I don't think Luke's family is interested in anything that has to do with us getting back together." She sat up straighter, placed a hand on her belly. "And if it weren't for the baby and protecting their mother, they would have kicked me out of this town already."

She had a point, but there was a hole in her logic. "I'm family, too." His voice gentled. "And that's why I'm here." Not with the Donovans' blessing *or* knowledge but once he developed a plan, he'd see if they'd buy into it. His wife might have a thought or two about the implementation of the plan, adding her own flair to it, but he'd be okay with that. What mattered was keeping the truth from Rose and getting Luke to settle down long enough to consider his options—did he really want to spend the rest of his life without Helena? That was an answer Tate intended to find out, but first he had to make sure Helena was willing to fight for a chance to be with the man she loved, even if he hated her right now.

"You're very kind." Her lips pulled into a faint smile. "Luke's comments about you don't match up to what I've seen."

That made Tate laugh. "Not surprising." He bet the guy's surly attitude was about the car Tate drove into town on his twenty-first birthday: black, loaded, lots of chrome. He'd wanted the car dealer to remove the price sheet from the back window, but Tate had been in a hurry and the guy forgot. Luke Donovan was a motorhead who loved anything with an engine and speed. It was Tate's bad luck the guy happened to step out of the Cherry Top Diner that summer afternoon at the exact same time Tate parked outside. Yeah, he didn't like to think about the rest, but that's what sat at the center of the guy's animosity. *You think you're a hotshot because you got this car?* he'd said. *It's always about money with you people, isn't it?* Tate should have kept his mouth shut but when the guy started in on his mother and sister, that was it. *You know what your problem is, Donovan? You're jealous; you've always been jealous and from where I'm standing, it's always about money with you.* Tate should have stopped there but, of course, he didn't. *Now leave me alone and go back to your miserable, punk-ass life.*

"It must have been hard for you to marry into a family that wasn't thrilled about your wealth."

"Hah." That was a true understatement. "The Donovans are proud, hard-working people, but sometimes they get blinded by that and assume those with money have never known struggle. Most of my life, I've wished I were like ordinary people. You know, without the cook, the gardener, the fleet of cars, and the unlimited credit cards."

Helena nodded. "All I ever wanted was to be part of a family and when I lost my parents a few years apart, I started to write. The first notes were sad and about loss because I wanted to honor my mother. I named the card line Annabelle Grace Cries. Annabelle was a heroine in a book I read about a young woman who could see the future and change it, ten years at a time. I loved that character and wished I could be her. Grace was my mother's name. Later, I started writing about love and caring and finding that special someone. What did I know about any of it? It was make-believe but I held onto it because I wanted to believe it *could* exist."

Tate nodded. "For too many years I didn't think there was such a thing as real love, especially after witnessing my own parents' sad relationship. They were more of a merger. And marriage? No thanks, not in my universe." His voice softened, and he thought of his wife and how she'd shown him just how wrong he'd been.

"But then you met Charlotte," Helena said, studying him.

"Oh, yes, then I met Charlotte." Tate frowned as he recalled the disastrous first part of their relationship. "It was a tough climb, but it was all worth it." The frown relaxed, morphed into a smile. "Definitely worth it."

"I'm really happy for you, Tate." She paused, her cheeks coloring with pink. "You're a good man and you deserve to be happy."

"Thanks." He'd never been comfortable with compliments, probably because there'd been so few in his life. Growing up in a household with Harrison Alexander where every single accomplishment was a lesson and a critique for the next effort had made Tate shy away from praise. "So...about the greeting cards..."

She shook her head, pressed her fingers against her temples. "Right, about that. Like I said, it started out as a way to express my feelings after my mother died, but when my brother and sister told me I could be a part of our parents' legacy if I wrote cards for the company, I agreed. I dreamed and wrote and watched my thoughts turn into greeting cards that people could relate to and understand. When Dominic and Estelle told me that sales had spiked and the line they created for me was selling well, I was so happy. I thought it would draw us closer together, make us a real family who cared about one another. When they asked me to create more cards, why wouldn't I do it for them? I wanted us to be a family...but that didn't happen..."

Tate studied Helena, pulled in by the heartache of belonging to a family who chose the bottom line over their own sister. Why did some people think the only thing that mattered was the next dollar? Did they not see it was about caring and relationships and doing the right thing by your family *because* you were family? "It must have been very hard for you."

She shrugged, cleared her throat. "All I wanted them to do was treat me like I mattered, like I was their sister and not some machine spitting out words. But the more I wrote, the more they wanted. Instead of making me feel closer to them, it distanced me. They asked me to transfer colleges after my freshman year and work closer to home. Oh, they said the environment was better for me and we'd see more of each other, but it wasn't about that at all." Her words swirled through the room, landed between them: sad, dejected. "It was all about making money. The more I created, the happier they were, and the more isolated I felt. But I wanted to please them, so I did it. I finished college, continued to work on the cards, and that's when I met my fiancé."

"Ah, the fiancé..."

Her voice turned hard and she spat out, "Right. Him. He acted so excited to hear I created greeting cards, said it was a true art. Right. He just saw the dollar signs and did the math. Money never mattered to me and I was so naïve. I thought he really cared about *me*, but all he wanted was my money and what it could buy him. A few weeks before the wedding, he spilled the truth and said he couldn't marry me because he loved someone else. Imagine that?"

"Jerk."

"Oh, yes. But guess what? While he told me he couldn't marry me, he could, however, collect the proceeds from the half of the house I'd signed over to him, the car I'd put in his name, the tailor-made suits... I paid for the wedding that never happened and the debts he left behind. That's what love got me and that's when I vowed never to trust a man again."

"And then you met Luke."

She closed her eyes, said in a voice coated with pain, "And then I met Luke."

~

HARRISON ALEXANDER DID NOT LIKE to lose. Had the man ever lost at anything? Camille doubted it, and yet there was a sadness about him at times that spoke of loss. How could that be? How could the man know what loss meant unless he'd cared about something or someone and lost?

Had he loved Marguerite despite his indiscretions? Camille couldn't say, and yet she doubted it. The man had never spoken of his wife with compassion or kindness. No, his references contained words like *inconvenient* and *overdramatic*.

No matter, Harrison would lose this time, and Camille would know the joy of unburdening herself from her husband. Carter could learn what freedom felt like if he joined forces with her and did what needed done. That's why she stood in Carter's rented condo right now, forcing a smile that pretended she could stomach him and his pregnant girlfriend. If they all joined together, they could beat Harrison Alexander: Camille would get her divorce, Carter would get his pregnant sex-toy, and Mindy would play at being Mrs. Carter Alexander.

Victory could taste so sweet.

She dug her stilettos into the carpet, placed a hand on her hip, and homed in on her estranged husband. "I have a strategy that will destroy Harrison's threats, and if you follow my plans, Mindy may even gain his acceptance." Camille eyed the girl whose pregnant belly stuck out in a shrink-wrapped top, revealing the results of Carter's inability to keep his pants zipped. She cared less right now. All that mattered was achieving her goal of uncoupling—a goal that required assistance.

Mindy clutched Carter's arm, stuck her pointed chin in the air, and said in a voice laced with possessiveness and suspicion, "Why should we trust you? Why would you want to help us now when you've tried to break us up tons of times?" The pointy chin inched higher. "You smeared my name in front of the whole town, so nobody comes into the Cherry Top Diner without staring me down."

It was obvious Mindy was the one to convince. Carter was simply the good-looking mouthpiece with no courage or insight. Camille started in. "I'm tired of letting Harrison dictate what the people in this town do and don't do, what his family can and can't accept, who we marry and who we love. Aren't you?" She homed in on the girl's pale face. "I've devised a way for Harrison Alexander to not only acknowledge you, but accept you. And by accepting you, he'll have to accept the child."

Carter attempted a smile, failed. He'd have to work on that smile if he were going to convince the town and the patients who were leaving his practice with the steadiness of a dripping faucet, that while he might have made a mistake and disregarded his marriage vows, he *did* love the mother of his unborn child. There could be no willy-nilly tepidness, no uncertainty when he made that claim, or he'd be considered weak and unbelievable.

"May I sit?" Camille eyed the cream leather couch, a low-end version of the one sitting in her living room at home. Hmm. Interesting. Carter's handsome face turned three shades of red as he nodded and scooped up gossip magazines from the center of the couch.

"Have a seat, Camille." More red darkened his cheeks. "Can I get you a drink?

Oh, but she should give him a break and ignore the clutter and shabbiness of the place, but she couldn't. There was a part of her that wanted to say, *See what you're missing, jerk? See what you gave up?* But she didn't, because maybe he didn't think he was missing anything. Maybe he really did love Mindy. "No, thank you. I'm fine." She eased onto the couch, folded her hands in her lap.

So?" Mindy plopped on the couch beside her, tucked a strand of limp hair behind an ear dotted with several studs. "Carter told me we should listen to what you had to say, but if you're just going to be mean, then you can leave now."

Well. Talk about little Miss Superiority. Camille tilted her head, studied the girl. The long hair needed to go, the dark eyeliner, too. And the clothes? Did the girl really need to advertise a bulging belly with a skin-tight top as though people wanted to see *that*? Her gaze slid to the chipped nails, took in the rows of costume jewelry circling her wrists, the heart necklace dangling between her breasts on a silver chain. Goodness, this was going to be a lot of work. Still, if the effort gained her a divorce, it would be worth it. Camille pulled her lips into a thin smile and said, "I'm offering you a chance to fill my spot."

The girl let out a laugh that shot straight to Camille's brain. "I've already filled your spot." Mindy rubbed her belly, tossed a knowing smile at Carter. "Didn't I fill her spot, babe?" Another laugh, followed by a sultry sigh. "And then some."

"Mindy." Carter shook his head, a warning that his girlfriend did not heed. He shook his head again. "Please."

Mindy rolled her eyes, flopped back against the leather couch, and folded her arms over her belly, pushing her breasts out to reveal a scrap of red lace. It was Camille's turn to shake her head; some things never changed. "If you want a chance to make people in this town forget how you two got together and eventually accept you as a couple —" she unzipped her handbag, pulled out a folded sheet of paper "— you're going to have to change a few things." Camille unfolded the paper, dug around in her satchel for her reading glasses and put them on. "The first section is for you, Carter. No more flirting with other women, no suggestive looks, no sexual innuendoes, no—"

"He doesn't do that!" Mindy spat out, turned to the man in question. "You don't do that anymore...do you?"

Oh, but this girl had a lot to learn about the man sitting next to her. Of course, he did it, had done it for years, and if someone didn't hit him over the head with the reality of his dead-end future if he didn't change, then he was never going to stop. Carter was like a hound dog on the hunt: his nose always going after the next scent. Nature versus nurture, or whatever you wanted to call it. Camille called it lack of control and lack of consequences. "Carter? Do you still do that?" She watched him bend his head and rub the back of his neck, a sign that he was deciding what and how much to reveal. Did Mindy recognize this for what it was?

The neck rubbing ceased and he lifted his head, laid a hand on Mindy's and said, "No. Of course not."

Which could mean—anything. Camille shrugged, turned back to the list. "Good, because this plan won't work if you don't cut off all extracurricular activities." She paused, let the silence accentuate her meaning. "We want the people of Reunion Gap, who are also your patients, to gain trust in you, believe you're a stand-up man who will do right by your...significant other and the baby."

"Significant other?" Mindy laughed. "*I'm his girlfriend.* His one and only. His one true love. His—"

"I get it." Camille narrowed her gaze on the woman. She really had no clue... "You're all of those and more, but nobody will look at you that way unless you give them a reason to...and that requires you and Carter to work together—with me."

Mindy sat up, laced her hand through Carter's. "I'm listening. What would we need to do?"

Oh, so now she had her attention. Most likely because of the acknowledgment that indeed she was Carter's one true love. Ahem, if the naïve woman believed that, then let her. Camille wanted this divorce and while she'd give these two the tools to carve a place in this town as a couple, she would *not* take sides or play mediator. Carter had a choice and for once in his fifty-some years, he would have to make it without the help of his brother. She flipped the reading glasses on top of her head, smiled. "We're going to make you a couple the town accepts. How do we do that? Carter, you'll spend time honing that charm of yours on your patients for the purpose of retention only. You'll use those brains of yours to write articles for the newspaper, offer talks at the library, *anything* to get yourself in front of the town and show them you've changed. No more flirting, no more arrogance, no more foolishness. Humble and contrite is your new image, and you *will* do it if you want a chance to keep the designer-label lifestyle you so enjoy."

"He'll do it," Mindy said, sliding a glance at Carter who sat next to her looking bewildered and out of his element.

Camille nodded, turned to the young woman. "You'll get a makeover. I'm not just talking about changing your clothes or makeup; I'm talking about a total makeover." Camille studied the limp hair, the string of studs climbing up her ear, the heavy eyeliner, the shrink-wrapped top...the high boots that said *cheap* and *no class*.

"What kind of complete makeover?" Mindy tilted her head, homed in on Camille's diamond bracelet.

"Everything and anything. We'll work on speech patterns, posture, mannerisms. The way a woman walks and holds her head says a lot about who she is and what she represents. You must always be mindful of that and choose accordingly. People will be observing, never forget that." She tapped a finger against her chin, flipped her glasses on her face, and scanned the list. "We'll go over music and television selections, food choices..." Camille removed her glasses, pointed them at Mindy. "If you want acceptance, you have to learn to play the game. Once you've undergone your transformation, you get to decide how much you want to keep and what you want to discard. You'll work with my friend Nicki Price. She's a transplant from Chicago, closer to your age; knows all about style and fashion. Great businessperson. The people in Reunion Gap love her, love her husband, her kids, even her dog. Wouldn't you like to have that kind of admiration?" Camille knew the exact moment she'd sold Mindy on her proposal.

"I would," Mindy said, her brown eyes wide, her voice filled with awe. "Nicki Price will work with me?"

Yes indeed, Mindy was interested and willing. All Camille had to do now was reel her in. "Of course, she will. We've already talked about it. You see, she's my friend and you can learn a lot from her." Time to drop the final nugget. "Maybe one day she'll be your friend, too."

The rest of the meeting fell together with ease as Mindy gushed and sputtered over Nicki Price and all the wonderful things the woman could do. *Carter, baby, she can make me look like a movie star.* And *Carter, sweetie, Nicki Price wants to work with me. She's from Chicago. She's beautiful and classy and she can make me look like that, too.* On and on it went, as Camille nodded, smiled, and jotted down notes, while Carter shifted on the couch, cleared his throat, and attempted to look interested. Too bad for him. He wanted Mindy? He wanted a young thing and a new family? Well, now he was going to have one, and if he wanted to continue to live in luxury, then he'd do what Camille said.

She'd helped him with his PR nightmares and guided him on ways to improve his image, but he *was* going to give her the divorce. They were meeting with the lawyers next week to sign the final papers. Of course, she'd continue to help them because she'd given her word, and Donovans never went back on their word. However, if he decided to chase another skirt or return to his old ways and jeopardize his chance of redemption, she'd let him sink. He'd lose his patients, his practice, his precious Mindy. Let him see how many women wanted to be with him when he had nothing but an overblown smile to offer.

Chapter 16

Camille's next mission involved an afternoon meeting and coffee with Rose Donovan during which she planned to share Lester Conroy's findings about Luke's *wife*. *Wife* was a loose term and an incorrect one, as Rose would discover soon enough. She hadn't seen Rose since she'd told Luke the truth about Helena, but she'd called her and left a cryptic message. *It's done. No need to worry about Luke anymore.* She'd been a bit surprised when Rose did not return the call to inquire about the details, though when she considered her sister-in-law's fragile nature, it made sense that she might prefer a face-to-face conversation.

Still, the lack of a response seemed a bit odd. Camille sat in Rose's kitchen, sipping fresh-brewed coffee and sampling a slice of lemon pound cake. Spending time in the kitchen had always been a balm to Camille and, with Carter out of the house, she didn't need to sneak around when she wanted to whip up a dish. She eyed Rose over the rim of her coffee mug, said in a quiet voice, "I thought I would have heard from you by now."

"Was I supposed to return your call?" Rose's brows pinched together, her blue eyes narrowed. "I did receive your message, but I must admit I was a bit confused. I'm not sure I understand what you were talking about."

Goodness, Rose *did* look confused. In fact, Camille wondered if the doctor had increased her medications or if she hadn't been sleeping. Maybe she was going through another bout of guilt and melancholy over Jonathan's death. It could be any or all of these and adding Luke's predicament might not be a good idea. Still, Rose *had* inquired and hinted that she had her own questions. Was it not Camille's duty to answer them? "We talked about Helena's background, remember? We both wondered about it, and I told you I would find out more."

"We did?" Rose rubbed her temples, her expression a mix of confusion and distress. She'd once confessed that her brain became a jumble when faced with difficult situations and it was often hard to sort out. Was that what had happened? Had the concerns over Helena's background been so much for Rose that she simply refused to address the problem?

"Yes, we talked. I was going to do a little investigating…" Better not say too much until she determined Rose's mental state.

"I don't recall." Her voice switched from confusion to a burst of joy, and that joy spread across her face. "Did you hear that Luke and Helena are going to renew their marriage vows? Yes, indeed they are." She nodded her dark head, blue eyes bright, lips pulled into a wide smile, so different from the Rose Donovan of five seconds ago. "Martin Olanski will officiate, and I'm almost finished with Helena's wedding handkerchief. Oh, but I can't wait. I worried so about Lucas, all those years of never knowing if he'd find his place or the woman who could settle him down and heal his troubled heart. But Helena's *the one*." More smiling, more joy bouncing from her face to her small hands as she raised them toward the ceiling. "Jonathan will be so pleased. Our troubled boy has been found."

Camille could stomach no more than three bites of lemon pound cake and a few sips of coffee before she excused herself, saying she had an appointment she'd almost forgotten. That wasn't exactly true, but she did have an urgent meeting that needed to take place, as in *now*. She called Tate, informed him she must speak with him immediately regarding a delicate matter. Thank goodness, he was not on an appointment. Ten minutes later, she strode into the large office that had once been Harrison's. Tate belonged here, a symbol of integrity, goodwill, and trust, so unlike his father, who'd possessed none of those. She squared her shoulders, headed toward the massive desk where her nephew sat, and plunked her handbag on it. "We've got a problem. A massive one that's about to land on top of us all."

Tate stood, made his way around the desk, and hugged her. "Massive? Land on top of us? That does sound serious." He pointed to the couch across the room. "Why don't we sit, and you can tell me all about it?"

What was it about her nephew that calmed her, made her feel as though the worst calamity could be rectified with the use of care, caution, and a logical approach? The Alexanders were lucky to have Tate, and though they might not recognize it yet, the Donovans were lucky, too. Camille sank onto the couch, clasped her nephew's hand. "Oh, Tate, I do believe Rose has had a relapse and I'm not sure what to do about it."

"Why do you say that?"

She did not miss the caution in his voice, a caution that said he already knew there was a situation, and now he wanted to know what *she* knew about it. "It's about Helena. Apparently, Luke spilled everything to Charlotte, Rogan, and Elizabeth."

"And?"

Darn, but her nephew knew when she was holding back. "Luke also told them I was the one who initiated the investigation into Helena's background."

Those silver eyes narrowed, filled with disappointment. "So I hear. I hope you didn't tell Rose."

"No, I intended to but when I realized her fragile state, I changed my mind. I'm really worried about her, Tate. Something's wrong. She's talking about Luke and Helena's wedding vow renewals and how she can't wait and is so happy that he's finally found someone."

She shook her head, drew in a deep breath, and pushed out the rest. "She's making Helena a wedding handkerchief and acting like Jonathan's sitting next to her. What are we going to do?"

"We? Aren't you the one who stirred up the trouble? Went behind everyone's back and hired an investigator to dig up details you had no right knowing? Luke and Helena love each other, and now it's a big mess. And I'm sorry, but you did them no favors."

"Me? I was trying to help Luke. I love that boy, and I'd do anything for him. I could not let a stranger come into town and hurt him."

"Really? Do you remember Rogan and Elizabeth? She was a stranger and she hurt him and look at them now. They're so damn much in love you almost need sunglasses to watch them. And they're having a baby and life is good." He dragged a hand through his perfect hair, the brackets on either side of his mouth deepening. "And what about me and Charlotte? Was that not the biggest catastrophe there ever was? I can't imagine life without her even though I had to go through hell to get to this point. But you know what? I'd do it all over again a thousand times to have a minute with her, and she feels the same way."

"You're different; so is Rogan. This is Luke we're talking about. Why would the woman lie to him? Why would she pretend to be someone she wasn't and why would she fake her own marriage? None of it makes any sense, and it was my duty to find out and let him know."

"It was your *duty* to support him, no matter what. Eventually, the truth would have come out because Helena would have told him, and they would have dealt with it. But guess what? You stole that chance from them. I don't know if it's because you don't believe in love anymore or don't believe in other people's happiness or have been so soured by your own marriage that you think nobody can truly love another person, but this is all on you. The only thing I want to know now is what you're going to do to make it right."

Camille blustered her way through another five minutes of conversation that included indignation and denial and ended with a huff and a refusal to accept she was the one who'd destroyed their chances. "If their love was true and strong, they'd be able to survive. I *saved* him from years of heartache. One day he'll thank me." And with that she stomped from his office. She'd almost made it to the elevator when Frederick Strong stopped her.

"Camille? Do you have a moment?"

She clutched her handbag to her side, sucked in a tiny breath. After the first session at Victor's Ballroom Dancing, she hadn't seen him again. Perhaps her less-than-kind remarks about his trustworthiness had driven him to quit or choose another day—one in which she wasn't present. "Frederick, how nice to see you." Camille raised a brow, waited. "What can I do for you?"

"I believe your intentions are honorable, but I also believe you're looking through jaded glasses and can't see the truth, even when it's staring back at you with crystal clarity."

"I have no idea what you're talking about." He stared at her as if to say, *You know exactly what you've done, and you know exactly what I mean.* "Well? Is that all?"

His lips pulled into a thin line and he stepped back—away from her. "Yes, that's all. One day, I hope you'll realize that not everything in life is a scheme or an attempt to harm another. Kindness and compassion still exist, as does love, but you have to open your eyes and your heart to see it. Goodbye, Camille. I wish you well." And with that, Frederick Strong turned and left, leaving her with too much to think about, none of it good.

LUKE COULD PRETEND he didn't care about Helena or he could pretend he did care. It all depended on his audience. If his mother was in the room, then he forced a smile and casual conversation as though nothing had changed between him and the woman he'd thought was his wife—the one who was carrying his baby. When Charlotte, Rogan,

Elizabeth, or even that pain-in-the-butt brother-in-law of his was around, he put on the tough-guy routine: tossed out a scowl, shrugged, and if forced to speak, kept it cold and brief.

Haven't thought about the future.

Still shell-shocked.

Can't say.

Who the hell knows?

And if they wouldn't let up, he knew how to stop them. Worked every time. All he had to do was open his mouth and let it fly. *How the hell would I know? Why don't you ask her?*

Of course, he tried to keep his anger under control, but he failed every time. Rage crept into the words; at least that's what Charlotte called it. But there was something else there, too, though nobody had noticed, or if they had, they weren't saying. Luke recognized the damn thing for what it was and no matter how hard he tried to force it from his words and his damnable brain, it wouldn't go away. Pain. Pure. White-hot. Scalding. He'd have to work on that. A few hundred more hours of practice and he might almost be able to hide it.

Or not.

How was it that a guy like himself who'd faked his way through a chunk of his life now struggled to make it through a half-hour dinner without the room closing in on him? Stupid question. He knew why. Knew her name, her scent, the way she tasted... Luke mumbled a curse. He didn't want to pretend anymore. Hell no. He wanted to drag the lies out in the open and set them on the table next to the pork tenderloin and tell his mother there was no need to teach Helena how to make homemade applesauce, or pumpkin pie, or biscuits, or any of his other favorites because she wasn't going to be doing *anything* for him—other than birthing the baby they'd created and learning to share it.

Luke sucked in a breath, blew it out nice and slow. The baby hadn't drawn its first breath in the real world and the tug of war for attention and time had already started. What if she tried to leave Reunion Gap and head back to Colorado or California? What if she didn't care about being close to his family? Letting the kid spend time with his or her cousins? Play with Tate and Charlotte's dog? The what-ifs kept him awake most nights and he refused to think about the fact that maybe he couldn't sleep because he missed Helena's soft breathing and warm body next to his. No, he would not consider that possibility.

He'd been careful to avoid situations where he might be alone with her and risk a barrage of questions, or worse, the look she sometimes gave him that said she was hurting as much as he was. *That* he did not want to see, so he worked long hours at Rogan's, making sure he was home for enough dinners to not rouse his mother's suspicions, and once the meal was over, he was off to his brother's again. *Working hard to get the place decent before the baby comes. Yeah, it's looking great. No, I don't mind.*

Why would he mind burying himself in work when the alternative was misery and memories he wanted to forget? And when he crawled into bed at night, exhausted and sore, what did it matter? It wasn't like there was anything waiting for him... Luke wasn't fool enough to think they could continue like this, living as though they were still together, still planning a future filled with love, hope, another child or two, even a dog. That was all gone now and if he thought about it for more than a minute, he wanted to yell. And then he wanted to get good and drunk and forget he ever met Helena Montrey, but how would he explain *that* to his mother?

Rose Donovan was the reason for the continued pretending. If not for her fragile emotional state, Luke would have spilled the truth about the woman he'd thought was his wife, and then his mother would have understood why there would be no marriage vow renewal. No future together, either. No anything. But Rose *did* have issues and the delicate balance between reality and fantasy sometimes wavered and made her world hard to navigate. That's why his mother was planning the damn marriage vow renewal as though it were the event of the year.

As though he and Helena were the perfect couple.

"Dear, is everything all right?"

Rose's soft voice pulled him back from the torment that had become his life. Luke met her gaze, offered a puny smile. "Lost in another world, I guess." *One filled with fake wives and piles of lies.*

She *tsk-tsked* him. "I told Helena I thought you were working too much. You're still newlyweds and your wife never sees you." More *tsk-tsking* and a dab of her napkin against her lips. "You need to spend time together before the baby comes because once that little bundle arrives, your whole world will change." Laughter tinkled from her, spread through the room. "You might not see each other for the next eighteen years."

Yeah, well, their whole world was about to change, and it had nothing to do with the baby. "I'll keep that in mind."

"Please do." Rose nodded and glanced at the woman next to him, who'd grown very still. "Helena, please keep an eye on my son. He needs his rest and while he won't listen to me anymore, I can tell he'll do anything you ask."

Silence. And then "I'll do my best."

Right. As if she could get him to do anything. Not anymore. But at least she knew how to play the game; at least he could count on her for that. He decided to add to her comment with his own brand of torture. "See, Mom, no need to worry. My wife's got it all figured out." There was no missing the sharp intake of breath next to him that said she did not appreciate his sarcasm. But when he darted a glance in her direction and caught her watching him with anger and disgust etched across those beautiful features, he knew he'd gone too far. He held her gaze, refused to look away. Those whiskey-colored eyes narrowed on him, the full lips thinned. How many times had he tasted those lips? How many times had she—

"On second thought, Rose, I'm going to make sure Luke gets his rest tonight." She laid a hand on his forearm, the gleam of her wedding ring sparkling under the light. "I'm going to keep him home tonight." Those lips pulled into a slow smile. "With me."

Rose sighed, her soft words rolling over him. "I think that's exactly what he needs. Husband and wife time."

Luke jerked his arm away, pushed back his chair and stood. Husband and wife time? Did she mean sex? His own mother telling him to have sex? He blocked out the thought. Hell no. "I've got work to do. Rogan and Elizabeth's baby's coming whether the house is ready or not."

"People have raised children in a house under construction. Look at your father and me. Do you know how many years we were working on this place?" Rose's voice shifted, turned sorrowful. "I can't even remember, but it never seemed to get done. Still, those were the days..."

"Yeah, well, I'm not sure Rogan agrees with that."

His mother shrugged, set her napkin on the table. "Before you run off, I want to talk to you two about something. Helena said I had to ask you, so I'm asking. Mayor Olanski called this afternoon and said he's still waiting on the marriage information from Colorado." She shook her head, her blue eyes a mix of concern and confusion. "He said if you can't find the information by Monday, then you should just head down to the courthouse and do the whole thing all over again."

"What? What whole thing?" Maybe he could still wiggle out of this... But his mother's next words said there would be no wiggling out of anything.

"He said you should apply for a marriage license and get moving on it because there's a seventy-two-hour waiting period." Rose settled back in her chair, folded her hands in her lap and smiled at them. "That's just enough time to get everything in order for Saturday."

"Saturday?" What had he missed? "What's Saturday?"

His mother's laughter swirled through the room: light, happy, excited. "Saturday's the day you and Helena will stand before your family and pledge your love to one another." She paused, let out a long, satisfied sigh. "Forever and ever."

Chapter 17

Luke would rather haul shingles to the roof than have a face-to-face conversation with Helena—in his old bedroom—but the talk needed to happen and if he had to do it five feet from the bed where they used to make love, damn it, he'd do it. "So..." He blew out a sigh, dragged both hands through his hair, and paced the room. It was easier to keep moving so he didn't have to look her in the eye. "Looks like we're going to have to talk about this." When she didn't respond, he glanced at her, noted the rigid back, the pinched lips, the clenched hands. Ticked and not happy, no doubt about it. "Well?"

She turned to face him, but instead of answering, she just stared.

Now she didn't want to talk? She'd been after him since the fallout to talk and deal with what had happened. Of course, he'd refused, but then he would have refused life-saving medicine if she were the one administering it. But this talk was different; it was about his mother and damage control. "Helena." Her name burned his throat, stung his lips. "My mother isn't going to give this up."

"I know."

Was that resignation in her voice? If so, it would make it easier to spit out what he needed to say before he changed his mind. "She expects us to go through with this charade." He could not say *marriage*.

A nod and then "She does."

Great. Words that meant nothing. This wasn't exactly what he'd expected. Actually, he thought she'd pounce on him the second he closed the door and hit him with a barrage of pleas to talk about their situation. But she hadn't. Instead, she'd gone stone cold; the glaciers he'd seen in Alaska had nothing on her. Fine, just fine. "Since we can't produce any documents, I guess we'll have to head to the courthouse and apply for a license." A *marriage* license, but hey, why not pretend it was a license for something else? Yeah, they were both getting good at pretending...why not pretend around this?

"I'll call and see if we need an appointment. Just let me know when you're available."

Wow, she made it sound like she was scheduling a dentist appointment. Luke shoved his hands in his back pockets, fixed his gaze on the floor. Isn't this what he wanted? No emotion, no tears, no begging for another chance. No nothing. "Sure. Sounds good."

"Luke?"

His belly still did flip-flops when she said his name. Damn it, when was that going to stop? Crap, would it *ever* stop? He dragged his gaze to hers, forced a gruffness into his voice. "Yeah?"

"Are you sure this is what you want to do? I know you're worried about your mother, but..."

"But this is a real marriage as opposed to a fake one?" When she nodded, he shrugged. "My mother can't handle the truth, not yet."

"But at some point, we have to tell her."

Was that misery in those words? Luke homed in on her face, tried to pick out the emotions, but she'd buried them so deep, he couldn't see anything. "At some point." He paused, added, "If you're not comfortable with this, then you need to say so now." Of course, he had no idea what he'd do if she didn't want to go through with it...

"It's not that at all." She sucked in a breath, said in a quiet voice, "What happens after next Saturday? Where do we go from there?"

So, she couldn't say *after we get married* or *after the wedding* either. "I'm not sure I understand." What a lie. He understood what she was asking and that was the problem.

Her cheeks turned pink, her voice wobbled the tiniest bit. "We'll be married for real and as far as your mother and the rest of the town is concerned, we'll be husband and wife. And then there's the baby." The pink on her cheeks spread, her voice cracked. "I don't know how we're supposed to keep pretending we're a couple."

Exactly. That was going to be a huge problem and he didn't have any answers. He was beat up, disillusioned, and tired, and if he could rewind his life, maybe he'd have asked more questions when he first met Helena instead of ignoring the spaces in her story. But he hadn't asked because he hadn't cared, and he'd never in ten million years believed she'd lie to him.

And look where that foolishness got them? He would not be foolish or trusting again. Luke opened his mouth and spilled out words meant to protect him from ever getting hurt by this woman again, even if the words weren't true. "Here's the way I see it. We'll share a house and the baby, but the open-up-and-bleed-for-me stuff? That's done, not happening." He sucked in a breath, finished with "Same with sharing a bed. Those days are over."

"I see."

"Good. Glad we understand each other." He turned to leave before he changed his mind and asked why she'd become so agreeable. Part of him wanted a fight, at least a few more questions. Anything but the dead space between them and the lack of emotion. That wasn't the Helena he remembered. Had he done that to her? Forced her to withdraw so deep inside herself he couldn't find her? Luke made it to the door, had his hand on the knob when she called to him.

"Luke?"

He swung around, faced her. She moved toward him, the shirt clinging to her middle revealing a small bulge where their baby rested. When she was an arm's length away, she stopped. "I'm so sorry we've come to this. I'd hoped with time, you'd at least consider giving us another chance, but I see the truth now." Her voice shifted, filled with regret. "You're not the kind of man to forgive someone who's betrayed your trust, no matter the circumstances. So, I ask only that you consider how next Saturday will affect us because life in the same house with a partner who isn't really a partner won't be as clear-cut or easy as you may think." She paused, licked her lips. "It could destroy us both and I'm not sure we'd survive it."

∼

HE WASN'T COMING. Luke had changed his mind and wasn't going through with it, even if it meant telling his mother the whole sordid tale. The Donovans were a strong family and they'd be there for their mother, no matter what happened. Just as they'd be there for their brother, even if they didn't agree with his decision or his behavior.

Helena sat in a living room chair, tried not to notice the sympathy on everyone's face. Rogan stood in the corner wearing a dark suit and pale blue tie. The man had checked his watch three times in the last five minutes. She guessed that's what brothers did when they realized they were about to witness a disaster and couldn't do anything to stop it. Elizabeth clutched his arm, the other hand resting on her very large belly as she leaned toward him in a gesture Helena had begun to notice that meant unity, love, and family. Charlotte and Tate did that, too, whether they were talking from across the room or sitting next to each other. The action was almost imperceptible, but Helena noticed it, as someone does when her own situation is lacking.

Rose hurried about in a flurry of green taffeta, a pale pink rose corsage pinned to her dress. Poor, dear Rose. The woman did not deserve the disappointment that was about to happen. Helena wished it could be different, had *tried* to make it different, but Luke Donovan was an unbending man. She clasped her hands in her lap, noted the nakedness of her wedding finger. She'd removed the ring last night, placed it in a box, and handed it to Rose saying something about not wanting to jinx herself by holding onto it. Luke hadn't worn his ring since the day he learned their marriage wasn't real and when his mother had asked about it, he'd told her that in his line of work, it was too dangerous to wear a ring. Of course, that was true, but she'd guess it was also true that he had no desire to ever put it on again.

Charlotte and Tate sat next to each other on the couch, thighs touching, holding hands, whispering in each other's ear. Love and happiness swirled about the room, clung to everyone but Helena, the bride-to-be. Mayor Olanski busied himself patting Winston and chatting away as though the dog understood every word. She'd never owned a dog growing up but could see the value of having one to provide comfort, compassion, and unconditional love.

Rose said Camille Alexander had been invited but Helena doubted the woman would show. Why would she when she'd been the one who hired the investigator and revealed the truth about Helena? The woman must be delighted that her instincts regarding Helena's background had proven correct.

Rogan crossed the room, bent toward her, and said in a gentle voice, "Let's give him another few minutes and if he's not here, I'll call."

She nodded. There was compassion and kindness in the man she hadn't noticed before, but she saw it now. "Thank you." His smile reminded her of the old Luke, the one who promised they'd figure life out together—no matter what.

"I knew I shouldn't have agreed to let him change at my house." Rogan shook his head, muttered, "He'd better not do anything stupid. Damn fool."

"I think Luke will do exactly what he wants to do. Doesn't he always?" A tiny part of her waited for Rogan to tell her Luke did what was *right*, at least some of the time. But he didn't because they both knew nobody could persuade him to do anything he didn't want to do.

"I'm really sorry, Helena. I wish things could be different." He laid a hand on her shoulder, gave it a gentle squeeze. "We're all here for you. Please know that. We love our brother but you're family now, whether you have a ring and a name or not and we aren't going to turn away from you."

Family. That's all she'd ever wanted. If she could find one glimmer of happiness in this tragic situation, it was that the Donovans had accepted her as family. Her smile spread, filled her with hope for herself and the baby. "Thank you." The Donovans would see that they—

"Hey! Why all the sad faces? Isn't this a wedding?" Luke stood in the entrance to the living room, bright eyed, hair mussed, tie askew.

Had he been drinking? Oh, please, no. He spotted her, sauntered across the room, and stopped when he was a touch away. The smile he offered fell out in a lopsided jumble. "Well, hello there, beautiful."

Rogan grabbed his arm, said in a not too soft voice, "Damn it, Luke, have you been drinking?"

Luke thrust Rogan's arm away, spat out, "No. What kind of jerk do you think I am?" He tilted his head, studied Helena. "Are you ready to get married?"

"What the heck are you doing?" Charlotte clutched Luke's other arm, leaned on tiptoe, and whispered something in his ear. Whatever she said made him scowl, rub his cheek. Then his gaze skittered back to Helena, softened, and he held out a hand. "Let's go find the mayor so we can get this shindig started."

Helena eyed him, placed her hand in his. She should refuse. Yes, she should snatch her hand from his and walk away. What respectable woman would exchange vows with a man who'd needed to ply himself with alcohol to get through his wedding? But she couldn't just walk away. What about Rose? Who was she trying to fool? It wasn't concern for Rose that made her clutch his hand and walk with him toward Mayor Olanski. It was the small, almost impossible hope that Luke really *did* want to go through with the ceremony, and another equally almost impossible hope that his reason for doing so wasn't all about preserving his mother's sanity. Maybe there was a speck of hope that he *did* want to marry her for the chance to find joy again.

There was no fanfare with this ceremony, no violins or harps; just a soft background melody that sifted through the room, complemented the mayor's words as Rogan and Elizabeth stood next to Luke and Helena, a true testament to love and happiness. When it came time to exchange the vows, Helena met Luke's gaze and shared the words she'd written last night, ones that lived in her heart.

"Love did not exist before you
 Hope was but a dream
 Happiness a wish
 Joy an unknown
 Until you walked into my world
 Opened your arms
 And your heart
 Covered me in happiness
 Showed me joy
 Gave me hope
 Loved me."

When she finished, Luke cleared his throat, eyes so bright they glittered. She slid the ring on his finger, waited for him to say something. They hadn't talked about this part of the ceremony because she'd wondered if he'd even show up, and until ten minutes ago, was certain he wouldn't.

Mayor Olanski cleared his throat. "Luke, would you like me to fill in here?"

Luke shook his head, his gaze burning Helena. Then he reached into his pants pocket, pulled out a sheet of paper and read:

"Love, happiness, misery and sadness have all come into my life because of you.

 You saved me, you tortured me, you made me feel again.

Life will never be the same because of you.
You taught me about love and loss.
Taught me about hope and despair.
Joy and sadness blended with love and hope.
They forced us together, pulled us apart, made us whole.
Together.
Forever."

WHEN ROGAN HANDED Luke the ring, he eased it onto her finger, clasped her hand in his. And when Mayor Olanski pronounced them husband and wife, he leaned in, took her mouth in a kiss so gentle it tore at her heart. The moment shifted, and congratulations followed with hugs, toasts, and well-wishes for ever after. Helena watched as her new husband made his way to the liquor table and downed a quick shot, then another. He spent the next twenty minutes with a bottle of whiskey and Rogan's attempts to steer him from it.

Charlotte touched Helena's shoulder, eyes bright with tears. "Welcome to our family. As messed up as it is sometimes, we're all still family." She hugged her, whispered, "Don't give up on him, please. My brother loves you. He just doesn't realize it yet."

Chapter 18

When Helena was younger, before the ex-fiancé who'd shredded her heart, she'd dreamed of her wedding day. Would her gown be fitted with seed pearls decorating the bodice and the fabric hugging her hips like a mermaid? Or would it flow in a sweep of satin or taffeta, swirling about her as she danced, the train adorned with lace? And the color? White, cream, or perhaps ice-blue? The flowers would be calla lilies with a few roses tucked in because what was more romantic than a rose? The groom would wear one on the lapel of his black tuxedo and it would match the color of his vest and bowtie. Oh, yes, she'd had it all planned out, and the desire to live it had been so strong, she'd convinced the ex-fiancé— without much difficulty, which, in retrospect, made sense since he hadn't planned to attend the wedding.

But those wedding dreams had exploded the day her fiancé informed her he loved someone else. Gone were the dreams of seed pearls, satin, and calla lilies, a stark reminder that wishing didn't make it true. Like now. Helena stood in Rose Donovan's sunroom, taking in the signs of spring. Clusters of tulips, hyacinth, and daffodils burst in the gardens: yellow, red, pink, lavender, white, even a deep purple. Two forsythia bushes sprawled along the back corner of the garden, their yellow limbs graceful and delicate. Elizabeth had told her she and Rogan were married in the Donovans' backyard, and Helena could picture it. Of course, she could picture them exchanging vows just about anywhere because they belonged together...

"Hey. How are you holding up?"

Tate Alexander moved next to her, drink in hand, concern etched on his face. The man had the kind of looks and class that made a woman take a third look and catch her breath, but it was his compassion that made him special. He cared about what happened to other people, and he tried to help, even when it could cause him grief. "I'm doing okay." Not exactly, but he already knew that.

"You look beautiful. I like the T-length on you, and the lace. I knew you could pull off a lace overlay if it was the right pattern. The ivory's perfect with your hair and complexion." His lips pulled into a slow smile. "And you can never go wrong with pearls. The long sleeves are a nice touch, too."

"Thank you." How did he know so much about her dress? Charlotte had brought her two choices the other day, both similar, but she'd said it was a gift from *her*—an apology in the shape of a wedding dress. "You seem to know an awful lot about this dress. Quite a bit more than Charlotte, who didn't comment on the lace or the reason ivory would look good on me." She studied him as a possibility settled in her brain. "Now why is that?"

A dull red seeped through his tanned cheeks and spread to his forehead. "Maybe I helped a little."

"A little?"

Tate shrugged, slid her a look that said he did not like her questions. "Okay, more than a little." Another shrug, followed by a long sigh. "Camille and I picked out the dresses."

"You and Camille?" She guessed she could see where Tate might get involved. The man did love his clothes and he had a sense of style that Rogan and Charlotte did not possess. But Camille? The woman who'd ruined Helena and Luke's chance for happiness? That was impossible to believe. "I'm sorry, but your aunt would rather see me halfway around the world than marrying her nephew. She made that clear when she hired a private investigator."

"Don't think I didn't let her know about her ill-advised meddling." His voice shifted, turned cold. "There's no excuse for my aunt's behavior, but I do believe she's sorry. She's the one who suggested we find you a dress. I knew you wouldn't accept anything from her, and it would seem awkward if I gave you the gift, so we turned Charlotte into the messenger." His lips twitched, pulled into a faint smile. "If you haven't noticed, my wife is not familiar with clothing styles or designers." He cleared his throat as the blush deepened. "I'm a little addicted to it."

It was her turn to smile. "No kidding?" Helena glanced at the navy suit with the tiny gray pinstripe and the gray silk handkerchief in the breast pocket of his jacket. Style, grace, and flair—the man had it, no doubt about that.

"Just do me a favor and don't let the rest of the family find out, okay?"

Helena let out a small sigh. "Sure, but trust me, they already know. So, what about Camille? Where does she fit in? Was this her attempt at an apology?" And if it was, why would the woman ever think Helena would accept it?

"I don't know what it is, but I'm pretty sure she regrets ever contacting that guy. If she didn't think she was responsible for this mess, she'd be here right now, front and center, eyeing you in that way she has that assesses and dismisses at the same time." He sipped his drink, nodded. "My aunt's got a screwed-up life right now, and she let her disaster cloud her opinion on what constitutes happiness." A smile, a shrug. "Obviously, she should have minded her own business and realizes that now." He pointed to Helena's dress. "Hence, the wedding dress."

"And you got involved because...?"

Another smile, this one wider. "Because I can't resist a good design."

His confession made her laugh. "Thank you for your honesty.

Your secret is safe." Though one look at the man and anybody would know he knew his way around designer fashions.

"I'm sure you haven't noticed, but your husband's been giving us the evil eye since I came out here."

Helena glanced toward the makeshift bar and spotted Luke, glass in hand, gaze homed in on her in a look that said *annoyed*. She turned away. "My husband is more interested in what's inside his glass than who's talking to his wife." Sad but true.

"I'm not so sure about that," Tate said in a low voice. "In fact, here comes the groom. If you need me, I'll just be a shout away."

She smiled up at him, grateful he was on her side. For all his charm and style, something told her he would be a formidable opponent. "Thanks, Tate." Helena glanced out the back window again, waited for Luke to approach. Why had he shown up today? That's what she really wanted to know but she doubted he'd share that information. Maybe the better question right now was why had *she* shown up? As if she didn't know, and the answer did not make her happy. Darn it all, she wanted another chance with Luke, wanted to hear him say he loved her, wanted to spend the rest of his life with her, wanted—

"Married women shouldn't flirt with married men."

Helena ignored the pang in her chest as she turned and took in the glassy stare, the pinched brows, the thin lips; they spoke of annoyance and she was the cause of it. "Why did you come today, Luke?"

He ignored her question. "Stay away from Alexander."

"Tate?" She shook her head, disgusted with his comment. "He's just trying to be a gentleman and make sure I'm okay."

"If he comes near you again, that pretty face won't look so pretty."

"Don't you dare touch him." Helena planted her fists on her hips, glared at him. "This has nothing to do with Tate and you know it. Why did you come today? Can you at least tell me that? Only a fool would think you wanted to be here and nobody in this room is a fool." She paused, sucked in a breath. "Including your mother. Why couldn't you just have taken her aside, explained the truth, and saved us all from this charade?"

"Helena—"

"Let me finish. You could have told her what I did, and she might have stumbled, but it's better than seeing her son suffer. No parent wants to witness that." She pressed a hand against her right temple and massaged the beginnings of a headache. "We should never have gone through with this." She blinked hard, determined he would not see her cry. "Can't we both be honest for once and just admit this was a horrible mistake?"

"No."

One word that could mean anything. "No what, Luke? No, you don't want to listen? No, you don't plan to tell your mother? No, you—"

"No," he repeated, his voice hoarse, eyes so bright they looked silver. "No, it wasn't a mistake to get married." He moved closer, framed her face with his large hands. "No," he said again, seconds before he dipped his head and kissed her, coaxed her lips open.

The kiss tasted of whiskey and desire, and she wanted more. It had been so long since he'd touched her...so long since he'd been this close...

Much too soon, he pulled away, stared down at her. "Let's get out of here."

Helena glanced at the living room, spotted Luke's family—her family now—watching them and making no attempt to hide it. Luke had once told her his family could be annoying and way too nosy. That had not been an understatement. She turned to Luke, nodded. "Where will we go?"

"Mom booked us a room at the Peace & Harmony Inn." He shoved his hands in his pockets, cleared his throat. "I didn't know about it until fifteen minutes ago. If you'd rather not..."

Of course, she should refuse him. They had too many issues to deal with right now and jumping into bed would only complicate those issues. And she might be naïve, but Rose Donovan had talked about the honeymoon suite at the bed-and-breakfast enough times for Helena to know *that's* the room the woman had reserved. People didn't go to a honeymoon suite to sit and chat, and Luke's kiss a few seconds ago said he wasn't interested in talking either. Sex, that's what that kiss had been about and that's exactly what would happen if she followed him to the honeymoon suite. And then what? Tomorrow they'd be at odds again? Luke silent and distant, and Helena hopeful and waiting? Sleeping with him would only tear open the scab on her heart and create a fresh bleed. She couldn't do that. Not yet. Not until they settled their issues.

"Hey, why don't we forget it, okay?" His voice wobbled, fell flat like he didn't have enough oxygen to get the words out. He looked away, shrugged. "It was probably a bad idea anyway."

Yes, it probably was. Once he touched her again, she'd dream of a life with him, a family, a future. If he rejected her, what then? She didn't know, but she would not live the rest of her life wondering if this moment could have been a shift in their relationship, a healing that led them back to each other. She had to take that chance. Helena touched his arm, smiled when he turned to her, and said in a soft voice, "We should say goodbye first, don't you think?"

THE PEACE & HARMONY INN honeymoon suite was a romance lover's dream: red rose petals strewn on the bed, mounds of heart-shaped pillows in pink and white eyelet, a vase of fresh-cut roses on the dresser, and candles. So many candles, waiting to be lit.

Luke had said little on the ride here. He'd handed her the keys to his truck, muttering something about *just to be safe*, tossed their bags in the extended cab and hopped in. She'd hoped there'd be some sort of conversation, but he spent most of the drive fiddling with the radio and settling on a country station. Well. This wasn't exactly how she'd pictured the moments before they arrived at the honeymoon suite, but if it were anyone other than Luke Donovan, she'd say his behavior had to do with nervousness. Hah! She'd bet the man hadn't been nervous since grade school, especially around a female.

But when he set their bags on the floor of the suite and closed the door, he began checking out the room, developing a sudden interest in the shades, the heating vents, the refinished dresser, even the ceiling fan. He did not go near the bed but wandered into the bathroom, flushed the toilet, turned on the water in the tub... Helena inched toward the bathroom, found him splashing water on his face as though he couldn't get enough. When he caught her watching him, he grabbed a towel, wiped his face, and tried to act like every new husband checked out the honeymoon suite as though it were a home inspection.

"What? Why are you looking at me like that?" The pink flush on his cheeks had nothing to do with a rigorous towel drying.

Helena shrugged. "Nothing. Just curious about your interest in the plumbing—" she paused, pointed toward the bedroom "—and the rest of the suite."

Those pale blue eyes narrowed. "Safety is a big issue for a pregnant woman, and this is an old bed-and-breakfast. I just want to make sure there aren't any fire hazards...or other problems..." He rubbed his jaw, tossed the towel on the counter and said, "That sounded like a bunch of bull crap, didn't it?" When she nodded, he worked up a smile and shrugged. "Yeah, that's what I thought."

Okay, this was definitely nerves talking. "Luke? We have so many issues between us, maybe this isn't such a good idea." Maybe? Sharing intimacy with him right now was the last thing she should do —and the one thing she really wanted.

He moved toward her, touched her cheek. "I can't think straight when I'm around you. My head gets all jumbled up." His fingers trailed to her neck, settled at the base of it. "I can't think right now, and it has nothing to do with alcohol. It's you, Helena, it's always been you." He leaned in, cupped her chin, and placed a soft, gentle kiss on her lips. "I want you...so bad I can hardly breathe."

There were so many unspoken words between them, but in this

moment, there was truth. Helena eased her arms around his neck, pressed her body against his. Oh, but he felt wonderful, and it had been so long. "Luke... Oh, Luke..."

He pulled back, took her hand, and guided her to the bed. "You're so beautiful." He knelt, placed his head against her belly, his strong arms circling her waist. He murmured something, then stood and undressed her, kissing her naked skin, teasing, tormenting, making her burn for him. "I want you," he said in a ragged breath. "All of you."

Helena unbuttoned his shirt, reached for his buckle. "Yes." She opened his shirt, ran her hands along his chest, trailed kisses over his shoulder. "Oh, yes." There was no talking after that as they made love with the desperation and longing of two souls reunited. Pure, true, a union that spoke of hope and forgiveness, and filled the gaps that words could not. Perhaps this could be a new beginning for them...more honest than before. It would require Luke to open his heart again, but they were worth it. Weren't they? *Yes*, her heart whispered as she drifted off to sleep in his arms. *Yes*. But the next morning, Helena woke to an empty bed, the indent on the pillow beside her the only sign her husband had spent the night.

Three days passed since the night at the Peace & Harmony honeymoon suite. Helena waited for Luke to tell her he wanted to have the conversation they both knew needed to happen, but he didn't. He was absent from dinner, too, sparking his mother's concern that her son should stop working so much and spend more time with his bride. Tate and Charlotte showed up at the dinner table, a rarity these past weeks. Their attempts to keep the conversation going included Charlotte's colorful recounting of what had happened at the shop that day, and Tate's comments about why his wife should consider another line of work. She sniped at him, he laughed, and they always ended up leaning toward one another for a kiss.

That's what marriage looked like. *That's* what love felt like. They pretended not to notice the empty seat next to Helena, but that was like Winston pretending not to notice the sirloin on the kitchen counter. Life had taken a turn, and while Helena had hoped for a second chance with Luke, she'd begun to doubt whether it would happen.

The fourth morning after their wedding, Tate found her in the kitchen, toasting a bagel and fixing tea. He and Elizabeth were the ones who showed her the most sympathy, and maybe that was because they understood what it felt like to be on the outside of the Donovan circle trying to find a way in.

"I bought some cherries at the market yesterday," Tate said, leaning against the kitchen counter. "You mentioned you liked them..."

Helena stirred her tea, smiled up at him. "Thank you. I'll have some for lunch." She carried her tea and bagel to the table, slid onto a chair. "Busy day?"

"Busy enough. I'm meeting with the contractor this afternoon to go over a few more details on the house. The excavators are scheduled to break ground tomorrow."

"I'm really happy for you. Winston's going to be happy about his new home, too."

"And I'll be happy as soon as he realizes he's not sleeping in our bed." He let out a sigh. "That's not a picture I ever imagined. What happened to dogs sleeping in their own beds?"

What happened to husbands sleeping in their own beds? Helena shrugged, slid him a look. "You married a woman who believes that sharing her bed with the two loves of her life is exactly what you should do." She bit into her bagel, thought about the Golden retriever who would bound down the steps any minute. Dogs had such simple lives. They loved, forgave easily and often, and did not harbor resentment. Too bad humans couldn't learn from them.

Tate cut into her thoughts, pulled her back. "Charlotte and I want to help you. Elizabeth and Rogan do, too. Nobody's exactly thrilled with Luke right now. I think even Rose is a bit annoyed with him." He clasped his coffee mug between his hands, said in a gentle voice, "We all really thought you and Luke were back on track after the wedding, especially after your night at the Peace & Harmony Inn." A dull flush crept up his neck to his cheeks, making it obvious he did not want to have this conversation. "But...who knows what's going on in that guy's head? He never was one for calm or cool, and we're all sorry you're going through this. If there's anything we can do, we're here for you."

Chapter 19

Life held a lot of surprises, some welcome, some even expected. And then there were those surprises that flattened you because you'd never seen them coming. That was the sort of surprise Rose Donovan had just confessed ten seconds ago. She'd spoken the words, let them filter through the room and grab hold of Luke, and *still*, he didn't understand them.

He stared at his mother, frowned. "Mom, are you saying you knew the truth the whole time?"

Rose tucked the afghan around her waist and accepted the cup of tea he held out to her. "Of course, I did, dear. A mother always knows her own child even if he doesn't understand himself. You'll see." She sipped her tea, offered a faint smile. "There's nothing like a child to change your life in ways you could not imagine." The smile made her eyes sparkle. "No matter how old you are, you'll always be my child."

Luke sat on the edge of the ottoman, planted his elbows on his knees. They'd all worked so damn hard to keep his disaster of a "marriage" from her and make her believe he and Helena were living in wedded bliss. Yeah, hardly. All those nights sleeping alone in his brother's old bed, ignoring Helena's voice, her scent, her presence, their baby growing in her belly? The only way he could succeed half the time was to remind himself how he'd opened his heart to her and she'd lied to him. But that got old because some nights he had a hard time holding on to the anger. Some nights all he'd wanted was to hold her close, feel her breath on his neck, her soft skin next to his, her voice whispering into the darkness... And then he'd gone and done the unthinkable—he'd married her for real. "So, when did you find out?"

"When did I find out Helena wasn't who she said she was, or when did I find out you two weren't really married?"

The first question hurt, but the second one burned his soul. Luke dragged a hand through his hair, let out a long sigh. He was so damn tired of it all, wished he were back in Colorado working on houses, carousing, and living the life. Who was he kidding? What he really wanted was the woman he had thought was real, and the life they'd planned. Damn her.

"Lucas? Are you going to sit there with that frown on your face or are you going to answer me?" Rose set her cup on the table next to her chair, leaned forward and patted his hand. "Life is never easy or what we expect, but if we're with the right person, we can get through anything. And because I know you're wondering, I knew your aunt was having Helena investigated." She let out a long sigh, said in a soft voice, "If I had it to do over again, I would have spoken to Helena first and gotten her side of the story. I'm usually not so rash, though I certainly was in my younger days."

"I thought she was the right one, Mom, I really did." He let this one piece of truth slip out. "But turns out I didn't know her at all."

She shook her dark head, patted his hand again. "Does the fact that she's wealthy and could support *you* make her wrong for you?"

"No, the fact that she lied makes her wrong for me." Putting sound to the words made his chest ache.

"I know it's difficult to accept, but sometimes we lie for the right reasons. You probably know about Rogan and Elizabeth and the trials they had. She meant well, but goodness, when Rogan found out the truth, it tore them apart. Tate had a hand in it, but he also had a hand in getting them back together."

"Do we really have to talk about Mr. Perfect right now? I'm still not happy about him and Charlotte."

"Why? He loves her. Adores her, actually, and she feels the same about him. Do you ever watch them together? He never takes his eyes off her for longer than a few seconds and she's the same way." A faint smile pulled at her lips. "It's heartwarming to watch after their rocky start. Those two were so worried about getting hurt that they built walls and got caught up in their own tales. It was not a good time, but now look at them."

Yeah, he'd rather not. "Look, Mom, I know you mean well, but, this is different."

"Is it?" She touched his arm. "Oh, Lucas, you've been a fighter your whole life, even when it wasn't your fight. You were so afraid to trust anyone but yourself, and heavens, no woman was *ever* going to own your heart. And I'm guessing when Helena came along and threw your whole world off balance, you didn't quite know what to do about it. But you took a chance and trusted her, and you think she betrayed that trust."

Because she did. His mother was not going to see it his way no matter how much he tried to explain. "Does it really matter now?" He'd married Helena—for real this time—because he hadn't been able to tell his mother it was all a sham. Rose had been adamant about the damn ceremony and they'd all believed she needed it to help pull her through her dark period. Besides, a piece of paper and a ceremony didn't make a marriage.

"It only matters if you want to know the truth. She loves you and her heart is breaking right now." She cleared her throat, sniffed. "Don't you think it's a bit odd that she agreed to go through with this marriage? She knew this one would be real but from what I've heard, Helena was more concerned about you than herself." His mother tilted her head to one side, studied him. "I'd say that's not someone hiding from the truth; that's someone admitting in front of our family that she loves you and wants to be with you."

Luke's gaze narrowed on her. His mother did have a way of

reworking situations to make them turn into what she wanted. "She did it because she owed us, not because she wants to be with me." If Helena hadn't wanted to marry him back in Colorado when there'd been no pressure, why would she want to now, with his family eyeballing her every move? The answer was simple, even if his mother didn't want to see it, which she didn't.

"Hmm."

When Rose Donovan made that sound, it meant she didn't agree. Their father had warned them about it early on. *When your mother makes that little noise, it's her attempt to tell you that you don't know what you're talking about.* Luke crossed his arms over his chest, sighed. "Okay, okay, what?"

A tiny shrug, followed by a sip of tea. "I didn't say anything." She eyed him over her teacup.

"Right, but we all know you don't need to say a word to say a lot. Are you going to tell me, or do I have to start guessing, maybe call Rogan and Charlotte so they can guess, too?"

"Heavens, no." His mother sat up straight, her expression a mix of compassion and sadness. "Do you remember when you were about to turn twelve and Camille bought you a shirt for the birthday party?"

Luke made a face, scowled. "How could I forget? It was purple."

Her blue eyes lit up and she laughed. "It wasn't purple; it was navy with a lavender stripe."

He shook his head, remembering the designer polo shirt his aunt wanted him to wear to the party. "I only saw purple." And for a twelve-year-old boy who didn't like to wear anything but basic colors, purple, or *lavender,* as his mother called it, was not happening.

"Your aunt was determined to see you in that shirt, said it was a perfect match for your skin tone and eye color. I think she might have been right, and with your light hair and the sun streaking it to blond, well, nobody could argue the match."

Except him. "Mom, it was purple, and back then I only wore four colors: blue, green, red, and brown." He'd expanded his color chart since then to include black, white, and the occasional gray. Who needed anything else, especially if ninety percent of his wardrobe involved jeans?

"I understand, but you know Camille has never been one to ignore a challenge, especially if she thinks she's right."

His lips twitched. "I know the feeling." His aunt used to call him stubborn yet determined: a worthy opponent.

"She thought a new baseball glove would bribe you into wearing that polo shirt, but I knew better. No matter how much you wanted that glove, you were not going to wear that shirt."

He smiled. "You're right. Nothing was going to make me do it."

It was her turn to smile. "Indeed not."

Something in her tone told him she'd been waiting for him to say that. Luke shifted on the ottoman, cleared his throat. "Rogan wouldn't have worn it either."

She raised a brow. "I think he might have suffered through it for the baseball glove. Not you, though, which is why I know you *wanted* to marry Helena." Before he could dispute her comments, she went on, "You wanted that baseball glove for a year, but not enough to wear a navy and lavender striped shirt for two hours."

"So?" He did not like where this was going.

Her expression gentled. "If you really didn't want to marry Helena, nothing would have convinced you to do it, not even your worries about me. Deep down, you know that, just like you know you still love her, and that's what's causing you such distress. You have a chance to start over, nothing between you but the truth and love. Don't throw it away, Lucas. Please don't lose the best person that's ever happened to you."

Luke didn't realize anyone was watching him until he looked up from the workbench and spotted Tate Alexander in the doorway. Damn, the guy was like a cat, prowling around without making a sound. "What are you doing here?" He was not in the mood for Mr.

Perfect with the fifty-dollar haircut and fancy shoes. Come to think of it, the guy would bug the crap out of him even if he wore rags and had a shaved head.

Alexander moved toward him, inspected the fireplace mantel Luke had been working on. "Nice job. If you're interested in working on my place, let me know. You could use the same crew...maybe start your own business..." He rubbed his jaw as if considering how Luke might do this.

Luke scowled. "Doubt I could help; I've never built a mansion before."

That made the guy smile. "It's not a mansion. Your sister calls it a mini-mansion."

"Mansion, mini-mansion, castle...hole in the wall... Whatever." Luke scowled, turned back to the mantel and his nail gun.

"Right, well, a structure like that will keep a lot of men working and I'm guessing that would be a good thing for a man whose family's about to increase."

Luke didn't answer. Who couldn't use extra money, but at what cost? He didn't want anything he didn't earn, not from a brother-in-law or a wife. That last thought jabbed his brain, pounded his right temple.

"Okay, then I guess I'll offer the job to one of the other guys. Otto maybe."

"Otto? He's a kid. What does he know about contracts and building codes?" Luke shook his head, blew out a sigh. "You'll spend more time doing repair work than enjoying your mini-mansion." Another sigh, this one louder. "You really have no idea how the trades work, do you? You have to get reliable people you can trust who can do the job."

"Somebody I can trust, huh? That's why I asked you, but you're not interested."

The guy really could be a pain. "I'll think about it, okay?"

"Sure."

Luke stared at him. "Anything else? I'm on a timetable here."

"Just one more thing." His brother-in-law took a step closer, picked up a hammer, studied it. "Helena misses you."

"I'm pretty sure my wife is none of your business." He was not going to discuss Helena with a guy who considered a sport coat casual attire.

"Maybe not, but she just came to see me about a place..."

Luke stood, set the nail gun on his workbench. "What are you talking about?" Before the disaster that became their lives, they'd talked about renting or buying once the baby came, but that conversation was long since over.

"She's moving out, Luke. Said she wants a place for her and the baby." He shrugged. "At least that's what she said. No mention of you, though."

No mention of him? Helena was moving on without him? He'd done his damnedest to avoid her since the night at the Peace & Harmony Inn so he wouldn't have to think about where this marriage was going—or not going—but that didn't mean he was moving on without her. It meant he was confused and lost and trying to find a way back to the way things were *before*, and maybe he was a chicken shit... Okay, he *was* a chicken shit about confronting his feelings, but his mother had opened his eyes today and made him admit the truth—he'd *wanted* to marry Helena, and he wanted another chance with her because *he still loved her*. And the only way *they* could work was if he and Helena took the jump and opened up about what happened between them: the misery, the heartache, the pain. That was *not* something he looked forward to, but he wasn't fool enough to pretend they didn't have to trust one another again to have a shot at making this marriage work, and he'd spent the last few hours trying to figure out a way to broach the subject.

And now she was moving and leaving him behind? Had she given up on him because he'd been a fool *and* an idiot one too many times? Fear swirled through him, shot up his throat and spilled out. "She can't leave me."

"Then you better get back to the house because from what I gathered, she's packing up her stuff."

Luke ran out of the house, hopped in the truck, and sped down the road toward the woman who owned his heart. He *couldn't* lose her, no matter what he had to promise or how many less-than-desirable traits he had to change. Hell, he'd do whatever she wanted as long as she didn't leave him. He pulled into his mother's driveway, parked the truck, and sprinted to the front door, banging it open like he used to when he was a kid, anxious to get to the next adventure. This was not about an adventure right now; it was about life and a chance to live it with the woman who could make him a better person.

"Lucas?" His mother stood in the kitchen doorway. "What's wrong, dear?"

"Where is she, Mom? Where's Helena?"

Her face broke into a gentle smile. "She's upstairs."

He bounded up the stairs, thrust open the bedroom door, and spotted her sitting on the bed, pillow propped against the headboard, notebook resting on her thighs.

"Luke?" She set the notebook and pen aside, brows pinched in what looked like concern. "What's wrong?"

She wouldn't look concerned if she were really leaving him, would she? Luke moved toward the bed, sat on the edge of it. "You're too good and kind and beautiful... And why would you want to be with me, right? I treated you like crap and refused to see your side of what happened because—" his voice cracked, spilled his pain "—you broke my heart. Nobody's ever done that to me before, maybe because I never let them get that close. You were different. You were like the first snowfall or the perfect sunset. The more I was around you, the more I *wanted* to be around you, until you became a part of me." He stared at his hands, studied the gold band he hadn't removed since their real wedding.

"Why are you telling me this now?"

"Because...because..." He sucked in a breath, slid his gaze to hers. "Are you leaving me? Just tell me the truth, okay? I know I don't deserve you. Everybody knows that, but if you could just give me another chance, I know I could make it right." Her eyes grew bright, too bright, like the tears would come next. Tears of sadness. Damn, it was too late; she *was* leaving him. Luke looked away, buried his head in his hands. His stubborn pride had cost him the only woman he'd ever loved.

"Luke?" Her voice burrowed to his brain, spiraled to his heart. "I'm not leaving you." Pause and a long sigh. "But we've got to get a few things settled." She placed a hand on his back, rubbed it in wide circles: gentle, calming. "I won't live with someone who doesn't want to be with me or who shuts down when there's a problem. I've grown up these past few months and learned that if you don't have truth in a relationship, you don't have a relationship. And even those we love will hurt and disappoint us. It's just life, but that doesn't mean we quit on them. It means we fight through it and stick together. That's what makes a great relationship...a great marriage...a great love."

Luke turned to Helena, reached out and swiped a tear from her cheek. "I thought I would never trust you again," he said, his voice cracking. "But I have to if I want us to be together, and I do want us to be together...so damn much my chest aches. Please tell me you haven't given up on me—" he brought her fingers to his lips, kissed each one "—tell me you'll give us another chance to get this right. We can learn together; I know we can, but please, just say yes."

"Yes," she whispered. "Yes." She inched toward him until they were a kiss away. "Why would you think I was leaving you?"

"Because you went to talk to Tate. He stopped by Rogan's and told me you were looking at a place for you and the baby." He paused. "One that didn't include me."

"Why would he say that?"

Luke kissed her knuckles, rubbed his cheek against her hand. "No idea. You didn't say that?"

"I did...but that's not what I meant. I guess I refused to believe you'd give up on us and I wanted to have a place to look forward to, a home for the three of us. That's what the visit to Tate was all about—wishful hoping."

"Damn that guy."

Helena smiled. "We should thank him. If he hadn't massaged the truth a little, who knows how long it would have taken for you to talk to me?" Her lips twitched. "I could be in labor or the baby could be walking."

That made him smile. "From this day on, we're in this together, no matter what." He leaned toward her, placed a gentle kiss on her lips.

"No matter what," she murmured against his lips. "But we're going to have to talk."

More kisses. "I can do that."

Helena pulled back, stroked his cheek. "About everything, Luke, even the things that make you uncomfortable."

He nodded. "I know. I'll do it."

She smiled. "And open up."

"Agreed." He loved the way her eyes lit up when she was happy.

"No more accusations, and no more hiding truths because we're afraid, even when we don't think the other person will like them."

"Yes, absolutely agree."

His wife's smile spread. "Thank you."

"You're welcome, Mrs. Donovan." He eased her onto the comforter, lay beside her. "Do you have any idea how much I love you?"

"I think as much as I love you," she whispered, trailing a hand along his chest.

"And how much is that?"

"There aren't enough words to describe it." Her hand inched lower, settled on his belt buckle. "But I *can* show you, if you promise to do the same."

And they did...oh, yes, indeed they did.

Chapter 20

J onathan Michael Donovan. No surprise Rogan Donovan had named the child after his long-suffering, do-gooder, *dead* father. How was it that such a weak man could be held in such high regard when Harrison couldn't garner common courtesy? People feared him: business associates, his children, his wife. And well they should. What good was the worth of a man if he had no power?

Harrison blew out a long breath, eased onto the park bench and eyed the hospital entrance. His source said the child was born two hours ago, mother and baby were fine, no complications. The Donovans and associated family members were in attendance. That meant Tate was there, acting like one of them, as though he belonged. Damn the boy, didn't he understand he did *not* belong with those people, would *never* belong? He was an Alexander, not some lovesick puppy chasing after a woman who wore steel-toed boots and jeans with holes in them.

Harrison's source was proving quite valuable. In a matter of weeks, he'd gathered information on many of Harrison's contacts: former and current business associates, enemies, family members. Who would have thought Camille would devise a scheme to transform

Carter's mousy pregnant girlfriend into a young woman with flare and potential, or that Carter would find the guts to stand up to him? Of course, Camille was behind it all and while Harrison hated to lose, he did admire wits and strong will. Camille Donovan Alexander possessed both.

And what of Frederick Strong? The man continued in Tate's employ, which proved more disappointment than annoyance and had been spotted twice at The Oak Table having coffee with Camille. What was that all about? Hmm... If he closed his eyes and disregarded the man's diminutive stature and boyish looks, he might see where his former sister-in-law might find Frederick attractive. It was the cerebral connection, no doubt about it, and one that bore watching for future developments.

Harrison had been about to take a quick jaunt along the patterned walkway to stretch his legs when Camille exited the hospital, her small frame heading toward him in high heels and a designer suit. She was indeed an attractive woman with too much class and attitude for his brother. He'd be curious to see how she'd match up with Frederick Strong. "Well, well. If it isn't my ex-sister-in-law." Harrison stood, adjusted his tie, and moved toward her.

"Harrison?" She raised a brow. "Imagine seeing you here. Have you come to welcome the newest Donovan to Reunion Gap?"

He laughed. Camille knew he'd sooner jump in pond scum than spend time with the Donovans—Camille and Rose excluded. "That's what I've always liked about you. You've got sass. Too bad my brother never appreciated it." He motioned toward the park bench he'd just vacated. "Care to sit? I need to speak with you and this will only take a few minutes."

She eyed him with a look of someone who is used to sidestepping traps and less-than-sincere offers. A shake of her red head followed by a tiny huff and then, "I think I'll stand. Easier to make a getaway."

Clever woman. "I hope your uncoupling with my brother doesn't mean I won't see you anymore."

Those pink lips pulled into a scowl. "I hope that's exactly what it means, Harrison. You've caused enough grief and done enough damage to most of the people in this town, including and especially your brother. Helping him by enabling him and making him beholden to you is one of the cruelest acts of manipulation I've ever seen."

He rubbed his jaw, considered her words. "Manipulation? Is that what you call permitting my brother's lifestyle?" Harrison paused, added, "And yours? And what about your children's lifestyle? When did you develop such a conscience, Camille? Was it before or after your husband's fifth affair? Or was it the sixth, or maybe the tenth? *You* enabled Carter as much if not more than I did, and if it's honesty we're talking about here, then let's both be honest." He stepped toward her, said in a quiet voice, "You enjoyed the lifestyle enough to look the other way and do not pretend otherwise." While he might admire her, he was not going to let her play the victim. His words must have bothered her because she stumbled back, her face pale, lips pinched. When she was able to speak, the words that spilled out were not ones he'd expected.

"I have my own sins to repent for, but you will *not* be the one telling me what they are. Life has a way of making us pay for what we want the most, especially when we try to make bargains to get it."

He did not like her tone. "Do you have a point?"

"You know the daughter you ignored, demeaned, and treated with disregard? *I* have a relationship with her. Do you even know what that is?" she spat out, her eyes bright, voice smothered in anger. "Meredith is coming back to Reunion Gap and if you have any hopes of repairing your relationship with her, you're going to have to prove your worthiness."

How dare she speak to him in that manner? Had she forgotten the power he wielded, the depth of destruction he could create with a single phone call? Apparently, she had. Harrison sucked in three calming breaths, forced a smile, and said in a voice that matched the chill in the air, "Is that a challenge or a threat? If it's the first, take care that you've honed your skills. And if it's the second? Remember, everyone has secrets—even the Donovans."

EPILOGUE

T*hree weeks after the birth of Annabelle Grace Donovan*

"How are my two best girls?"

Luke eased onto the couch beside Helena and their baby girl, Annabelle Grace. "Perfect." She turned to her husband, smiled.

"Just like her mother," he murmured, placing a kiss on Helena's temple.

Soft. Sweet. Innocent. Seconds from now, his lips would work a path to her neck, taste the tender flesh at the base of her throat... And there would be nothing innocent about the kiss. Helena sighed, stroked Luke's hair. "I don't think this is a good idea." Not that she would ever tire of his touch or the desire to be with him. Those had intensified these past months, since the day he came to her, begging her not to leave him. Tate still caught grief for the scheme, but he and Luke had developed a bond, even if neither would admit it. "Luke..."

"Hmm?" He nuzzled a spot behind her ear.

"Did you forget your family's stopping by? Your aunt's bringing lunch and a dessert she swears is your favorite." Camille Alexander had apologized to Helena and Luke for what she called *irresponsible meddling* and had taken every opportunity to show how sorry she was and how much she approved of the marriage. A high-end stroller, a month of meals, and a salon day for Helena.

The kissing stopped, and Luke sat up, rubbed his jaw. "Damn, but can my family not leave us alone? You think it's great having them care so much?" A scowl, followed by more jaw rubbing. "How about caring *too* much and not respecting a husband's privacy to be with his wife?"

That made her smile. "If they didn't want to see Annabelle or visit, then imagine what you'd be saying? We did the same when Jonathan was born. You even learned how to change his diaper, remember?"

A slow smile crept over her husband's lips, followed by a laugh. "Yeah, I remember. I thought I did a pretty decent job, better than my brother-in-law who got his fancy silk tie peed on."

"Yes, there is that." The Donovans would never let poor Tate forget that one. "Maybe Tate and Charlotte will be the next ones to have a baby."

Luke stroked Annabelle's tiny head, said in a gentle voice, "If they do, they have no idea the kind of miracle that's waiting for them."

He was so right. Helena had imagined life after the baby, but the pure love she felt the moment she held Annabelle in her arms and every second after was incomparable. A true miracle that she hoped Tate and Charlotte would know one day. "Speaking of miracles, are my brother and sister still coming next week? They haven't called with a last-minute cancellation?"

He shook his head. "Nope. Dominic and Estelle will be here; trust me on that one."

"I hope you realize they're not coming to see the baby." She'd accepted their allegiance to business over family a long time ago, but it was hard to explain to a person who belonged to a family like Luke's.

Those pale blue eyes glittered with something that looked like a cross between determination and anger. "If they think they're going to fly in here and start negotiating a deal with you and Elizabeth, they can think again. Rogan and I have already talked about it." He glanced at their baby, eased his large hand down her back. "Tate's in on it, too."

"In on what?" Helena and Elizabeth had plans to create a card line together; Helena would provide the word content, Elizabeth would create the cover. The day after Annabelle was born, Luke contacted Dominic and Estelle to fill them in on a few details: their sister had a husband *and* a new baby. That hadn't impressed or surprised them, but when he mentioned the new card line Helena planned with her artist sister-in-law, *that* had gotten their attention and an airline reservation. *To see our niece, and meet you, of course*, Estelle had said. *We can't wait*, Dominic added and then he'd slipped in the rest: *Since we'll be in town, could we chat about the new line, maybe come to an agreement?* "Luke, what's Tate in on?"

He shrugged, his smile turning mischievous. "Let's just say if your brother and sister want to negotiate, Tate's lawyer's ready for them. I guess Fred Strong is tough and brilliant and doesn't cower to bullies. I hear he chose to stay with Tate rather than going with the old man. Anybody who can stand up to Harrison Alexander has my respect." The smile spread. "Plus, Tate says Fred has a thing for Camille. No idea if it's true, because I've got my own issues making sure I don't screw up again." His voice gentled. "And that's a full-time job."

Helena stroked his cheek, her chest swelling with emotion. "Thank you for caring so much. My brother and sister probably aren't going to change, and I'm finally okay with that. Do you know why?" Her voice wobbled. "Because I have my own family now. You, Annabelle, and all of the Donovans." She paused, added, "And Tate."

Luke's eyes grew bright, his voice hoarse. "We *are* your family and we're so glad you're part of ours." He brushed his lips over hers, whispered, "You're my everything, Helena Donovan." Then he eased back, cleared his throat, and pulled a scrap of paper from his pocket.

"I started this the night Annabelle was born but didn't finish it until this morning." Luke sucked in a deep breath, blew it out. "This writing stuff is harder than I thought. Okay, here goes:"

MY DEAREST LOVE,

 Life began the moment you looked at me

 the moment you smiled

 and opened your heart.

 Love entered my world

 gave me hope that happiness and joy could exist.

 Each day with you brings a newness to it

 and a smile filled with your love, your touch, your kindness.

 I did not know such a love could exist,

 until you.

 You touched my soul,

 opened my heart,

 and made me believe.

 We are separate, and we are one as we come together

 To live and love one another

 Forever.

 And always.

❧

MANY THANKS for choosing to spend your time reading *Lovers Like Us*. If you enjoyed it, please consider writing a review on the site where you purchased it. Reviews help readers decide which book to select next.

 If you'd like to be notified of my new releases, please sign up at http://www.marycampisi.com

ABOUT THE AUTHOR

Mary Campisi is the bestselling author of over 40 emotion-packed, romantic women's fiction novels that center around hope, redemption, and second chances. Set in small towns, these books take readers through the lives of the characters as they encounter, misfortune, disappointment, and challenges to find hope, friendship and, in some cases, love. Growing up in a small town gives Mary a real sense of how people pull together to help others find their true destiny. Her stories will make you laugh *and* cry, but in the end, you'll feel like you want to live in these towns, meet the residents for coffee or share a meal.

Mary's Truth in Lies series, also known as the *A Family Affair* books, takes place in the Catskill Mountains and centers around the discovery of a man's secret family that prompts the question, *Which family is the real one?* The continued success of this series is driven by readers wanting more and she's created an equally compelling one with the Reunion Gap series.

Mary should have known she'd become a writer when at age thirteen she began changing the ending to all of the books she read. It took several years and a number of jobs, including registered nurse, receptionist in a swanky hair salon, accounts payable clerk, and practice manager in an OB/GYN office, for her to rediscover writing. Enter a mouse-less computer, a floppy disk, and a dream large enough to fill a zip drive. The rest of the story lives on in every book she writes.

When she's not working on her craft or following the lives of five adult children, Mary's digging in the dirt with her flowers and herbs, cooking, reading, walking her rescue lab, Henry, or, on the perfect day, riding off into the sunset with her very own hero/husband on his Ultra Limited aka Harley.

If you would like to be notified when Mary has a new release, please sign up at http://www.marycampisi.com/book/book-release-mailing-list/

To learn more about Mary and her books…

https://www.marycampisi.com
mary@marycampisi.com

facebook.com/marycampisibooks

twitter.com/MaryCampisi

amazon.com/author/marycampisi

bookbub.com/authors/mary-campisi

Printed in Great Britain
by Amazon